D1138930

llantyne's Folly

s Ballantyne, proprietor of a failed sea-front hotel in West of England is an idealist who sees himself as a ruth-, calculating realist. He thinks of himself as a Field-Marshal ning his campaigns with people in place of Army Corps, visions and Battalions.

He believes himself to be hard-bitten. No Utopian ideas for n. He envisages a do-it-yourself scheme strictly on his home ound. This is to be a pilot for more ambitious undertakings. or is he prepared to let anyone or anything frustrate his plan the children. Not his brother-in-law's love affair, the lead-g town councillor's political ambitions, his love for his own ife Irma.

His scheme is to persuade a sick and beautiful widow to sell he local mansion, a huge Palladian structure, for tax reasons for a song to the local council to be converted into a school for the under-privileged children of the town. It looks plain sailing, a straightforward enough project, even though – and Ballantyne is not one to flinch from anything necessary to further his cause – it might even necessarily involve him in making sexual advances to the pantherish Mrs Fitzpayne. The advent of the mysterious but redoubtable Mr Buzbee soon alters that.

also by Claud Cockburn

Beat The Devil
Overdraft on Glory

A NOVEL BY

Claud Cockburn

Ballantyne's Folly

WEIDENFELD AND NICOLSON
5 WINSLEY STREET LONDON WI

SBN 297 00092 6

Printed in Great Britain by Bristol Typesetting Co Ltd, Barton Manor, Bristol

One

It occurred to me, forcibly so, that even though he was my brother-in-law the fellow ought to be wearing a white coat. Not a short one; that would have made him look like a bartender with a touch of the muscular gigolo. But why not a long white one, coming down to about the middle of his calves? That, surely, would have been suitable wear for the principal oculist of our town.

I was leaning forward with my eyes unnaturally wide open, trying not to blink.

'Pete, tell me, why don't you wear a long white coat?'

He had an electric lantern strapped to his head, which was as it should be. As an auxiliary, he held in his right hand a small, neat, but powerful electric torch which he shone into one or other of my eyes from time to time. Instead of answering my question, he went on shining and peering, and after a lapse of a second or two which made it appear that my question was really not worth answering at all, he said,

'I wish I could drink whisky at this hour of the morning and get away with it. For you as a hotel keeper it is admirable – encourages the clientele. For me it would be ruinous.'

At this I instinctively drew back my head a few inches, whereupon he swore at me softly, asking me for God's sake to hold still. I felt sure that his remark about whisky drinking

5

was simply a statement of fact, with no oblique criticism implied. I am accustomed to drink a good deal of whisky at some times, and wine at others. Therefore I am rarely aware of the smell of alcohol on other people's breath. But I am not so ignorant or self-centred as not to know that what is described as a whisky breath can be extraordinarily unpleasant, even nauseating, to a non-drinker, or to one who has not yet had a drink. I therefore convicted myself of gross incivility, amounting to actual unkindness, in having taken my normal morning drink just before making this visit to the oculist. For the plain fact was, and it should have been plain to me at the outset, that by the very nature of his job this man had been compelled to sit for a quarter of an hour or more with his nose only a couple of feet or so from my mouth. By my carelessness, I had brought an element of quite unnecessary unpleasantness into his morning's work. My heart went out to him. I sympathized with him in the nastiness I had brought upon him. I began to think of ways and means of recompensing him for the annoyance, to say the least of it, I must have caused.

It is easy to think of recompenses one will make to people in the future. The difficulty is to hit on something to do here and now. It seemed to me that the best I could do just for the moment was not to resent his off-hand treatment of my question about the long white coat. I therefore stopped resenting it on the spot. That might have left me stranded with nothing more to offer. But his manner as he continued to examine my eyes solved this problem. It gave me something more to forgive.

One could reflect that in fact Pete's behaviour in general, his whole physical activity, was a desirable contribution to the amenities. Old-fashioned people used to speak censoriously of what they called 'Showing Off'. This was simply a proof of their own failure to understand that everyone should exert himself to decorate life to the best of his ability. What, I asked myself, is the essential difference between a person who does his best to show off the beauty of his clothes and personal physique and the decorator who enhances the beauty of a room? I decided to repent immediately of meanly critical thoughts I had from time to time entertained about Pete in this respect. For example: when he dined with myself and my wife at the hotel I have often allowed myself to be irked by what, in cheaply derogatory manner, I had chosen to classify as a flamboyant display of physical charm. I had, in fact, been guilty of supposing that he was either 'showing off' to other guests in our restaurant, or else seeking to make a physical appeal to my wife, his sister. It had often seemed to me that the latter was the case. But suppose it were. What, looked at without prejudice, was wrong with that? So far as it went it could be said of course that it was a form of incestuous activity. If it were so, I decided now that I would forgive him that too. I was anxious to put no limits to my tolerant benevolence. What, in a civilized society, is actually wrong with incest? One knows that in primitive societies there are all sorts of excellent reasons for regarding this form of sexual relationship as taboo. Indeed, from a book which a visitor had left behind at the hotel, I had only recently learned the interesting fact that among the inhabitants of Cape York Peninsula in Australia the word Kuta-Kuta means both incest and cannibalism, deemed the most exaggerated forms of sexual union and the consumption of food.

It appeared to me that a question to him about his views on incest might elicit a better response than my two previous questions. I did feel it a pity not to have a small, general, civilized conversation about something other than the precise state of my eyesight. I was therefore about to say 'By the way, Pete, what do you think in general about incest? Do you think it is positively good, positively bad, or a matter of indifference, a marginal question without serious importance in our present society?' However, before I could do so, he jabbed a full stop on the paper with his pen and got to his feet in a lithe movement. He said,

'Well, that seems to be about it.'

He said he would not bore me with technicalities, but that briefly the situation was that I was becoming continuously more long sighted, that my eyes were not developing quite harmoniously one with the other, but that the prescription he was going to give me for new spectacles would provide all necessary adjustments.

This abrupt termination of our interview was something of a rebuff. I had not had the advantage of reading any full assessment of the incest situation and since I was childless and had neither brother nor sister, whereas Pete did at least have a sister, he might have been in a position to contribute some useful opinion such as I was not able to form for myself. But I had already made myself a nuisance. I therefore thought it best to let the matter go at that. Still, I had so far not given Pete any overt evidence of penitence and good will. He had no way of knowing that during the last ten minutes I had been repeatedly and vigorously forgiving him. And now was the time to do something more appreciable. I said,

'Look, if you have nothing better to do, why don't you come down to the hotel around quarter to one or one, do some diving in our pool, and then have lunch with Irma and me?'

In so far as the use of the pool was concerned he could of course have come without invitation. I instantly recognized that in fact my extension of the quite unnecessary invitation was a rather shabby attempt on my part to ease my sense of guilt. Perhaps, too, it was an equally shabby attempt to underline the fact that the pool was after all my pool. It was for this reason no doubt that I added the invitation to lunch. But as I left his office and walked the half-mile separating it from the hotel beside the bay, I made up mind to do my best to make this lunch something a little more festive than just another gathering of myself, my wife, and Pete. With Pete's example before me, I felt it my business also to exert myself to add to the amenities, the decorations of the day.

Pete's residence, as was seemly for a rising oculist, was in an area of town called The Crest. It was described as being 'exclusive' and was so, in the sense that anyone who could not afford the rents there was excluded. Even the local pub was more like a roadhouse than a pub. On its terrace, looking over the town to the sea, sat under coloured umbrellas stoutish, loutish men of leisure, middle aged or elderly, but gaily dressed and loudly spending time and money.

By these I was shunned. As proprietor of a sea-front hotel, I might normally have been accepted, even invited, to their clubby gatherings on the terrace. My predecessor had often been among them. I had sat there only once, after an appointment with Pete. In conversation with three or four of them at one of the larger tables I had spoken unsuitably; speaking, in fact, of the miserable conditions of the poor of our supposedly affluent town: in particular of the condition of the near-homeless and the children. They had, at the time, looked askance. Then one of them had 'made it his business', as he said, to make some enquiries about me. He reported that I was an ex-schoolmaster with 'something fishy' in my past.

As I went by, one or two of them gave miniature hand-wags, intended, no doubt, to be rather more chilling than a straight cut.

Our town had the qualities of a *coitus interruptus*. Nothing, however hotly desired, was pushed to its full and natural conclusion. The sea front and promenade had a timorous kind of garishness. Successive generations of speculators had started out to renovate, to keep up to date with contemporary notions of what a sea front should be. Each had lost courage or impetus half-way through, with the result that the scene was a series of desolate and hideous compromises. History remained always a discouraging jump ahead.

The same was true of the new office buildings which, as a result of official dispersal programmes, were occupying larger and larger areas of what might have been housing space. They made their surroundings look lower and meaner than they were. But they themselves, as though suddenly convicted of presumption, abandoned any attempt to attain the elegance which a proper height and full use of their materials might have given them. They were like thalidomide babies spawned by genuinely modern buildings.

On the morning of this interview with Pete, I said as much

to a few men gathered in the saloon bar of a pub in that mean section of town between The Crest and the sea front. Many of the streets here carried out, in their own fashion, the town's yearning for compromise. About a third of them could be classed, though naturally they were not classed, as slums. But here and there, amid the mouldering, over-crowded relics of a Victorian resort, someone had managed to retain or acquire and decorate an entire dwelling. Such a dwelling made it possible for people to cry out in protest when anyone did in fact dare to describe the place in general as a slum area.

The particular bar into which I now turned was known – had for years been known – locally as 'the Kremlin'. There was another down the road, frequented by Irish immigrants, which was dubbed 'the Vatican'. At one time I had found the atmosphere of 'the Kremlin' sympathetic. In contrast to those at The Crest the habitués did speak, often and vehemently, of the real conditions in our town. On accidentally discovering this, I had thought that here I could both acquire first-hand information about those conditions, and also put myself in touch with those who were not only victims but rebels. Only a couple of weeks ago I had suggested a mass march on the Town Hall. I was a little drunk at the time, and elated by the thought that these people would understand my feelings. I spoke of the ease with which it would be possible for resolute men to overcome any impediment or resistance offered by the police.

Now, this couple of weeks later, a discouraging thing happened. The place was empty except for the barman. I conversed with him for a quarter of an hour. And at the end of it he conveyed to me, in a friendly though warning way, that in the opinion of the habitués of 'the Kremlin' I was some sort of police agent – a spy, or provocateur.

I was so much taken aback that I said, idiotically enough, 'But they must know I'm nothing of the kind.'

'But how would anyone *know* that, Mr Ballantyne?' he asked. 'How does anyone know a thing like that about anyone else, one way or another?'

I had to admit his point. I went on towards my hotel. On my way through the building, making for the garden and swimming pool, I stopped to look at the visitors' book. At that time of year this is normally no more than a gesture. I was a good deal surprised to see that two guests had, in fact, registered. The names were illegible. In the column showing where the visitors had come from, the word 'Ireland' was clear.

In my office I mixed myself a highball and, carrying it, went on towards the pool. I should mention that this can be said to be the only distinguishing feature my hotel has. It is, as far as I can see, the only reason why anyone should stay at my hotel rather than at one or other of the similar hotels in the bay area.

Two

It was not necessary to be a guest of the hotel in order to make use of the pool. Anyone could do so on payment of an entrance fee. The amount of this fee had been the subject of debate between myself and my Norwegian wife, Irma, when we first took over the hotel. That there had to be some sort of fee seemed to be indisputable. Otherwise there would be nothing to deter people who had time to spare but no convenient place to sit or lie down, from putting in their time just sitting or lying on our lawn: perhaps not even availing themselves of the opportunities for healthful exercise offered by the pool. One could picture a situation arising in which such people, who could well have been accommodated on the public beaches, would actually crowd out athletes in training, people seeking to retain their health by the exercise of swimming, children being taught in safety the elements of this useful and delightful skill, and other elements of the community whom one should encourage to the best of one's ability.

The actual number of shillings to be asked was a different matter.

It had seemed to me that to set it as high as Irma originally suggested would be to exploit the supposed rights of private property in a manner which could be denounced as anti-social, and indeed would be apt to be so denounced by me. The entrance fee, I felt, should be only just high enough to give pause to the purposeless lounger of the type I have referred to. To impose a higher tax on this pleasure presented itself to me as an uncivilized act. At that time Irma enjoyed any opportunity to exercise her newly-acquired English. She also enjoyed argument for its own sake. She now produced one which I have occasionally heard used by people too mean to give sixpence to a beggar, or too lazy to stop and fumble for such a coin in their pockets. Irma, on the contrary, was activated not by meanness but by an unbridled enthusiasm for the welfare and swift advancement (if necessary by revolutionary means) of the majority of the human race. This enthusiasm was heightened, but in my view somewhat distorted, by an insufficiently thorough examination of what, under given circumstances, makes a society tick.

'So what!' she had shouted. 'Charge them the earth! Prove to every working, sweating son of a bitch that a heated pool is for the rich alone, not for the likes of him and his under-privileged brood. Tear the deceptive mask from the face of our so-called affluent society, our egalitarian democracy! Show,' she cried, putting spurs to her English and shaking it into a rousing gallop, 'show beyond a peradventure and without fear of successful contradiction that whereas the rich can possess a first class television set and yet swim in comfort whenever they want to, the working man is meanly forced to a choice between the two.

'Let him realize that if he decides in favour of the television set, still regarded by some as a luxury, but in reality a necessary part of a full modern life, then the heated pool is beyond his reach. He and his children may shiver in the cold waves of the open sea. They may catch their deaths of cold. One or more children may be sucked out by the undertow common along this coast, and drowned before it has learned the elements of swimming. Or, if these dangers are to be avoided, the family must resign itself to spending its leisure either in the cramped quarters of some dingy council house, in the beery stench of the saloon bar, the sickly air of the seaside tea shop, or squatting wind-beaten and risking piles, upon some expanse, cheap but nasty, of damp sand. By such means you will bring them face to face with reality. You will raise their social consciousness to the *nth*. You will send them in marshalled and militant ranks to demand the drastic overhaul, or total overthrow, of a system under which such iniquities are possible. They will,' she concluded, ' get a move on.'

I had thought it unnecessary to animadvert at any length upon the errors inherent in this argument. Apart from strictly political considerations, the reasoning was morally flawed. What right had one, I asked, to condemn people to the conditions she described on the assumption, for that is what it came to, that such sufferings would in the end do them good? It was that sort of false reasoning, falsely attributed by villains to progressive and forward-looking people everywhere, which often did grievous harm to the very cause which men and women of goodwill had at heart. After further argument back and forth we fixed on a fee of five shillings for adults, half a crown for children.

Irma had to admit that for this sum the paying customers could probably be said to get their money's worth. The pool was in the centre of a spacious lawn, which itself constituted an oblong promontory extending into the bay and washed on three sides by the salt waters of the sea. The fourth side of the lawn was formed by a spacious and gently sloping bank, declining from the narrow terrace at the back of the hotel, to the lawn.

When we took the hotel this bank had been an uneven mass of rubble with weeds sprouting wildly among heaps of tin cans and old bottles, while here and there a few abandoned shrubs dragged out a stunted existence in a state of undernourishment and actual disease. This horrid scene had seemed to me at the time an ugly, if trite, warning of what Nature, plus the detritus of modern society in the shape of can and bottle, may combine to bring about in the way of desolation. The former owners of the hotel had displayed this ugly wilderness without comment and, so far as I could see, without shame.

Probably shame had been swallowed by despair years before. Their only reference to it had been the statement that ' It's no use trying to grow anything so close to the sea. The salt kills everything. Poisons the air. Poisons the soil. No good trying to grow anything at all.'

In this statement there was of course a small element of truth. Irma however regarded it as contemptible, defeatist. Her understanding of horticulture was both profound and extensive. She know not only what sort of plants might be expected to flourish under these conditions but why they would do so. To enlarge her own knowledge she obtained from horticultural journals and other sources the addresses of such gardeners, wherever they might be in the world, as could be expected to have experience of gardening successfully, even grandly, beside the sea. Owners of famous private gardens, park-keepers, landscape gardeners on the coasts of Britain, Ireland, the Baltic, the Northern Mediterranean, Central New Zealand, and suitable areas of Japan received from her thoughtful letters and returned expertly thoughtful replies. To the transformation of that wilderness she devoted a considerable part of the 25th, 26th and 27th years of her life. She spent money: not, as the cost of beautiful gardens goes, a great deal, but enough, given our circumstances, to be nearly ruinous.

This appeared to me well worth while.

The delicious result was not produced mainly by money. It was achieved by energy. But there was more than energy. The success was brought about by a combination of creative art with a powerful and extensive grasp of scientific possibilities and limitations.

The scar on the face of the earth had become grandly and beautifully herbaceous. Its upper edge and sides were decorated with flowering shrubs at once delicate and flamboyant. Once a Japanese came all the way from Kobe and visited us. There were, he told us, only twelve things he wanted to see in Europe, and one of them was Irma's garden.

Looking at the matter from what is called a strictly practical point of view, which is sometimes a helpful, if limiting, angle of vision, it may be said that in the matter of the paying customers there was one obvious advantage and one equally evident drawback to the arrangement.

Except at the very height of the season the number of guests staying at the hotel was rarely more than a fifth of the number it was equipped to accommodate. For quite long periods we had no guests at all. Thus, if use of the pool had been restricted to hotel residents the aspect of the pool itself and of the surrounding lawn would have been melancholy indeed. To see Irma's garden unappreciated by any eyes other than our own, to contemplate the vacant pool and calculate the fearful cost of its heating apparatus, would have been lowering to the spirits. By admitting outsiders we could ensure that on almost any day of the week there was some sign of human life in and around the pool. And at week-ends there were sometimes as many as forty persons there.

This was the advantage I speak of.

The drawback was that in order to reach the pool visitors had to enter the front door of the hotel from the street, and pass through two long corridors on the ground floor on their way to the door opening on to the terrace above the bank. During this transit they had an opportunity to examine, if they chose, the state of shabby disrepair into which the furniture and other appointments had fallen. Many of them did take this opportunity, as I knew from overhearing their disparaging comments as I sat in my office opening off the second corridor.

There was another feature of this passage through the hotel which could properly be described not so much as an opportunity but as an experience to be inevitably suffered. These corridors stank.

By some trick of the draughts, which even on days when the weather was mild seemed to pierce the hotel's interior, the smell of inferior food being prepared in the ill-found kitchen, or gently decaying in the overfilled garbage bins, would have remained pungently disagreeable to a person who had been sitting inside the hotel smelling it for hours. Upon anyone entering directly from the fresh air of the street it had the effect of a sudden attack with noxious gases. This too was naturally the subject of loud remarks by the intending swimmers.

Disturbingly often I overheard parties of motorists who had been attracted by the advertisement of our pool congratulating one another on having been, as they said, 'warned'. They now knew that there was at least one hotel which they need not consider as a possible temporary residence. They would also be in a position to warn any friends who might be thinking of making holiday at our town against taking rooms with us. It was, as I say, disturbing: the more so because it was quite evidently impossible to alter the factors producing the situation without major, and possibly damaging, adjustments to the whole structure of one's activity. Time and mental energy are neither of them limitless.

On descending the steps cut in the bank and emerging on to the lawn I noted with pleasure that, although this was the morning of a week-day, there were already two strangers seated beside one another, hand in hand, on a cane-covered, cushioned settee beside a low table at the pool's edge. As I paused in a casual manner at the foot of the steps, a brief glance at the pair on the settee sufficed to suggest to me that here, properly handled, were the ingredients for turning a routine lunch into something rather more unusual.

The pair consisted of a man with a mop of silver hair and a girl or very young woman. The man's silvered hair was probably misleading as an index of his age. His face in strong sunshine definitely indicated that he could not, unless one quite unnecessarily assumed that his face had been lifted, be more than a few years older than myself, I being forty-two years of age. His right, or disengaged hand, was performing elegantly vigorous gestures, while his left gently held the right hand of the girl.

The girl was of that type which causes the observer to ask himself seriously whether her apparent beauty is due to the vivacity which lights her face, or whether she would be equally lovely if stunned or sleeping. As I advanced slowly across the lawn she turned to see who was coming, stretching one arm along the back of the settee, and I saw that her figure was excellent even in relative repose, from which I deduced that the same would probably be true of her face. Just before reaching them I made a final observation of a startling nature. The girl was a younger replica of my wife Irma: the spitting image, as the saying goes.

Almost at first sight I had made up my mind to scrape acquaintance with these people with the idea of improving for Pete's benefit the quality and interest of my lunch party. At that earlier moment I had been prepared to find that they wished to keep themselves to themselves. Indeed the holding of hands and the quality of the looks which passed between them as the man talked and gestured, certainly suggested that this might be just what they would be eager to do. But on noting this strange accidental resemblance to Irma I naturally determined to force my company upon them. It was too interesting an accident to be left unexplained in the interests of conventional politeness or reserve.

However no forcing tactics were necessary. I had hardly reached the table and greeted them with a small flourish and rattle of the ice in my whisky glass when the man bowed in the most affable manner and rose gracefully from his seat. His clothes were as elegant as his gestures. His strong, square face was of the kind into which, in earlier days, one might have expected to see an eyeglass screwed.

Sentences of a banal but warmly civil character were exchanged. I said I hoped they were happy. They said they were indeed. And the girl said, 'Apart from anything else how could we be unhappy with a garden like that to look at!' Fearful that their geniality might suddenly evaporate, leaving me high and dry, I decided to engage their interest further.

'The garden,' I said to the girl, 'was made by your double.'

She said, 'Explain, explain.'

The man said: 'Of course explain, but sit down do. Perhaps it will take a long time. I hope so, personally I prefer long stories to short ones.'

I sat down and said: 'But before anything else, surely you want something to drink?'

'As a matter of fact,' the man said, 'we did order something at the bar as we came through. Perhaps the waiter didn't understand we were going to drink it out here.'

I explained to them that the waiter in question was not really a waiter; or rather that this was his first job in that capacity. He was by profession a jockey. A combination of circumstances had compelled him to leave the turf abruptly. Existing under a heavy cloud he was prepared to work for very low wages. This was naturally an advantage for us. Very low wages were all we could afford. On the other hand hardly anybody except ourselves would in the particular circumstances have employed him at all. Before coming to us he had worked very briefly as an electrician at a local garage. He had been accused of pilfering and dismissed. Fortunately I had barely concluded my explanation when the man himself came at a bandy-legged gait across the lawn with a tray and glasses. His expression was one of shifty bewilderment. I had not yet made up my mind whether this was produced by the pressures of his novel employment, or resulted from his experiences when questioned by the stewards of the Jockey Club, and, more recently, on a lower level, by the garage proprietor.

Wishing to show the strangers that despite the appearance and smell of the corridors our hotel still offered certain amenities even in addition to Irma's garden, I said to our waiter with some sternness,

'How often have I told you that when guests order whisky and soda to be brought to their table, it is absolutely wrong for the waiter to bring whisky ready poured in glasses, and a syphon, but no bottle of whisky. That may be common practice in England, although it is not so in the United States. You must surely see that it is in itself discouraging and leads later to repeated interruptions of the conversation while somebody has to go off and order new drinks. Please now fetch the bottle.'

'Admirable,' said the man.

'Goody,' said the girl.

'And now,' said the man, 'the explanation about the creator of that wonderful garden.'

'I have to disappoint you,' I said. 'I have no explanation. I simply stated a fact. The garden was made by my wife. Irma Nordahl was her unmarried name. She is Norwegian. If she were not some years older than you appear to be she would be your double.'

The girl looked at me with the expression of a child who has been presented with a delightfully interesting toy. The man watched her, taking evident pleasure in her appreciation of this unexpected gift. I said, 'But you must judge for yourselves. You will, I do hope, lunch with my wife, my brother-in-law and myself. I must tell you frankly that the food in this hotel is very far from first class. Naturally I don't warn all guests. It does seem to me that the really extraordinary accident of this resemblance somehow calls for some exceptional frankness on my part. Or don't you think so?'

'I appreciate that,' said the man. 'I agree with you entirely. Although it will be perhaps disappointing if neither I nor my wife see the resemblance as clearly as you do. That could happen. Different people's eyes can see things in astonishingly different ways.'

I remarked, perhaps rather irrelevantly, that my brother-in-law was an oculist.

Three

The irrelevance resulted from the derailment of my thoughts by the stranger's reference to the young girl as his wife. This had the effect of a shock or jolt, an agreeable one like that produced by a quick swallow of neat whisky. Unless both of them were heavily disguised (unlikely) she could not possibly have been more than half his age and, at least at first look, the difference seemed greater than that. It was possible to assess the situation in one of three ways, but however one chose to regard it, the matter had the stimulus of the unusual.

Passing the possibilities in review before my mind's eye, I reflected that (a) his statement might be true. But in that case it was an unusual marriage. Or (b) she was not his wife but his mistress. In that case she was a shining example of a near nymphet. She had, perhaps, a touch of gerontophilia, the passion for a much older man quite often, I have been told, experienced by well-sexed young girls. Finally (c), she was perhaps in reality his daughter for whom he cherished a more than normal paternal passion. I had to admit that this speculation was coloured, or biased, by my earlier musings on the precise nature of the *rapport* between Peter Nordahl and his sister.

Friends have criticized me for what they are pleased to call a tendency to undue impetuosity, sometimes going so far in their indignation as to accuse me of outrunning the emotional constable by presuming on a certain degree of friendship to the extent of committing gross impertinences.

At a slightly earlier period of my life I would certainly have thought it suitable immediately to pose the questions frankly to my new acquaintances. I would have straightforwardly asked them whether (a) (b), or, speaking quite freely and candidly as among friends, (c) offered the correct answer. It would have seemed to me the obviously proper way to leap boldly over the barriers and obstacles which convention, like the organizer of a preposterous gymkhana, sets up to impede the progress of our relations with fellow beings, handicapping us in our race through life against the speed at which time passes.

But I had been, as the saying goes, chastened by past experience. To take one instance: I had often felt that the disclosure of financial irregularities on my part which brought to a sudden end my earlier career as a schoolmaster would have been less decisive had I not been regarded by colleagues and superiors as, in other respects too, a generally 'irregular' individual. Though to some it may seem strange in this day and age, I am almost positive that the headmaster's general view of me was unfavourably coloured by the purely objective and sociological interest I showed in his sexual attitudes. I heard much later that he had accused me of insinuating, in the course of several conversations with him, that he was a partially suppressed homosexual. In reality, I had simply been eager to get, at first hand, a clear picture of his sexual reactions to (a) his wife, a good-natured but plain woman some years older than himself and (b) the good-looking lads with whom he was brought into daily contact. One or two of them were, to my mind, uninhibitedly anxious to use their physical attractions as a means to procuring favours and advancements of one kind and another. I had no solid objection to that state of affairs, being simply anxious to clarify it in my own mind.

Having this kind of experience in mind, I now refrained

from putting to my guests the questions that presented themselves to me.

In the fraction of a second while I was deciding so to refrain, the stranger said, 'But we should introduce ourselves. My name is Buzbee, BUZBEE, Norman Buzbee. Edwina,' he said, turning to the girl, 'let me introduce Mr . . .'

'Ballantyne,' I said, 'James Ballantyne.'

We all expressed ourselves delighted at the encounter.

'I suppose,' I said to Mrs Buzbee, 'you are not by any chance Norwegian, or partially so?'

'Liverpool,' she said, 'Liverpool from way back. Absolutely no chance, I'm afraid, of some mix-up in a cradle under the midnight sun.'

'We are confronted,' Buzbee said, 'with a freak of nature.'

'Are you,' said Mrs Buzbee, 'suggesting that I and Mrs Ballantyne are freaks?'

'You are not freaks by any means. But the situation is freakish. Freakish by nature. Naturally freakish.'

On the man spelling out his name I realized that this must be the proper interpretation of the unintelligible hieroglyphics I had seen in the visitors' book. They were not passing visitors to the pool but had actually registered as guests of the hotel.

'And you sir,' I said, 'are from Ireland.'

'No,' he said, 'not really. Not at all.'

My interest was naturally heightened. It is not at all unusual for people to register at hotels under false names, and to give false information as to their place of origin. It was, however, of evident interest to meet a man who took the trouble to write down this piece of false information and then casually to state that it was indeed false. He spoke and gestured with animation.

'You understand, of course, that if one writes down the name of one's real place of origin, one may be inviting unpleasant intrusions on one's privacy. Let us say that some undesirable lout whom one scarcely knows and has been avoiding for years, come on holiday to this town and to this hotel. He glances at the visitors' book as he registers. He sees that someone from the same town is staying in the hotel. Being, *ex-hypothesi*, an undesirable lout, he chooses to regard this mere coincidence as a form of introduction. He makes a bee-line for his fellow townsman. He may even be someone one has never so much as met. It makes no difference. He obtrudes himself none the less. On a desert island such behaviour would be at least pardonable. In a seaside resort, visited by thousands yearly, it cannot be excused. But the fact that it is inexcusable does not make it any the less vexatious.'

'But to take your present case,' I said, 'suppose unknown louts turn up from Ireland? Coming from another country and across the sea, surely they will find even better excuse for claiming some kind of actual bond, and intruding upon you? And,' I added, 'take it from me that when, as occasionally happens, an Irishman is loutish, he surpasses in loutishness the members of any other race or nation I can think of.'

'You have a point,' said Mr Buzbee. 'It was careless of me. I simply failed to give the matter adequate thought.'

Bland is a correct description of his tone as he offered this explanation. He seemed, indeed, to be making it clear that he was not seeking to insult my intelligence by pretending that this was a true and acceptable account of the matter, but was simply asking whether, off-the-cuff or off-the-peg, it would make do as a temporary explanation. This mark of respect for one's intelligence struck me as endearing. It was the equivalent of trusting me, at least partially, with some kind of secret.

Farragut, the formerly renowned jockey, crossed the lawn with the bottle of whisky, followed by the appearance of Peter Nordahl. Stripped to the trunks for bathing, he was a notable figure of physical grace and strength, his muscles not bulging at all but rippling all over him. As he approached us I found myself awaiting with eagerness the effect upon him of a sudden recognition that Mrs Buzbee was the younger double of Irma. It seemed to me that psychologically this would be a moment well worth experiencing.

But in the event, nothing noteworthy happened at all.

He paused within a few feet of the table, acknowledged my introductions, bowed gracefully, and excused himself, saying that if he were going to do any diving before lunch he had better get on with it. He got on with it, using diving boards of ascending heights. But I noticed that on this occasion his diving style was perfunctory. It had nothing of the agreeable dramatic dash and show off which he invariably displayed when, for example, Irma was among the spectators of what, in those circumstances, I thought of as his 'act'. Mrs Buzbee's vivaciously expressive face at once revealed that she, too, had been expecting some different reaction and was disappointed, not to say cast down.

With a small note of petulance in her voice she said, 'I think you must have been wrong about this resemblance between myself and your wife. Your brother-in-law seemed to have noticed nothing. And surely an oculist . . .?'

In time to assuage her disappointment, her words recalled to me the realities of a situation which I had foolishly forgotten.

'I think you are jumping,' I said, ' to a conclusion unjustified by the facts. My brother-in-law is an almost tritely obvious example of a physician unable to cure himself.'

'You mean,' interrupted Mr Buzbee, 'that he is short-sighted?'

'A victim of exaggerated myopia. When he bathes he leaves his spectacles in the hotel with his clothes. He has not, in any meaningful sense of the word, set eyes on you at all.'

' So we are left in suspense,' said Mr Buzbee.

Alone among those present I saw Irma approaching. She had come, not down the path to the garden, but round the corner of the shrubbery which terminated a few yards from the pool. Pete was crawling at speed, three-quarters submerged. The two Buzbees had their backs to her. Her tread was light on the delicately rubbery turf. Mr Buzbee was the first to hear it. He turned his head and it seemed almost in the same movement was on his feet stepping round the head of the settee and extending both hands to Irma, clasping hers in his and contemplating her radiant face with a well-blended mixture of delight and awe.

'My God,' he said, simply, 'you are Irma, and your husband is right.'

'Well, I'm so glad about that,' Irma said, and seemed to be waiting interestedly but without impatience for an explanation. Then Mrs Buzbee turned too and got to her feet. Irma looked at her quickly and said, 'Aha! I understand. Certainly James was right. Although it cannot have been very difficult for him to be right about something as obvious. I,' she said, her tone slightly defiant, as though this point required attention and emphasis, 'have known him to be right about much more difficult matters than that.'

My heart glowed with love and gratitude.

Irma directed at Mrs Buzbee a smile of excited happiness. 'What a coincidence,' she said. 'What a fine and happy accident!'

It occurred to me to remark, simply because the thought lumbered through my head at that moment, that, considered *sub specie aeternitatis,* or in the light of the totality of things, there was possibly no event which could properly be described as accidental. 'I doubt,' said Buzbee gravely, 'whether we know enough about what you call the totality of things to judge what is accidental and what not.'

Irma took a few steps to the edge of the pool and called out, 'Come out of there you porpoise! Lunch!' And as Pete thrashed his way to the side rail, she said, 'Just you wait till you get your specs on. We've got something to show you that will knock your eye out. You'll goggle through your goggles.'

And indeed as the four of us assembled for lunch in the decayed and smelly dining-room, it seemed that she had spoken no more than the truth. Pete, the Viking, could not conceal the fact that he was, as the saying goes, struck all of a heap. It is part of the business of a physician to give his patients the impression that however exceptional and dismay-

26

ing their symptoms may appear to them, he, from his superior peaks of knowledge, views them calmly and, above all, without surprise; his manner must imply that he had a pretty good idea of what ailed them even before they displayed their symptoms in the flesh. Many physicians, and Pete was one of them, are so used to adopting this manner in their business relationships that they go on wearing it in what is rather absurdly called private life. They put one in mind of an absent-minded doctor turning up at a ball, or gala reception, with a stethoscope still hung around his neck and bumping against his shirt front between the white tie and waistcoat.

But as he wagged his head and spectacles from Irma on his left to Mrs Buzbee on his right, Pete's simple and excited astonishment was evident to all. Myself, I felt that I had given him a real treat. I had fully made up to him the distasteful experiences to which I had subjected him earlier in the morning. Naturally, the impact of these two beautiful creatures, so similar, so nearly identical, except for a difference of a dozen or more years in their ages, was in a sense embarrassing, that was to be expected. But the embarrassment was like that of a man who, preoccupied with conversation, gulps a goblet of champagne under the impression that it is a still, white wine. The fizz makes his nose and eyes prick, and nearly chokes him. But a moment later comes the uplift, and with the second and third glass he feels his potentialities expand, sees splendid vistas opening before him.

In view of Mr Buzbee's flattening observations on the subject of accident, I had the feeling that it would be somehow unsuitable to pursue the matter further at that time. Buzbee himself seemed to consider the subject at least momentarily closed. He started immediately to discuss a news item we had all read in the morning newspapers. This concerned a family in North Wales, fatally stricken by a mysterious disease. In a matter of four days, the grandmother had been found dead in her bed, and three of her nine children had dropped dead after breakfast on three successive days. The remaining grandchildren, six of them, were in hospital for observation. The parents were prostrated by shock. The question was whether these grisly events could be regarded in isolation, as would be the case if, for instance, it was found that the inferior metal of their saucepans or frying pan had somehow poisoned their food.

Or they could have been eating something out of tins of which the contents had become contaminated, as had occurred some years ago with widely distributed consignments of Argentine canned meat. If this proved to be the case, the affair would be of some national importance. But it would still be quite possible to protect oneself against the menace by ascertaining as soon as possible just what type of canned food this unhappy family had eaten, and then taking care not to eat that sort of canned food oneself.

But there was a third possibility, cautiously hinted at by the newspaper reports.

It could be that this episode in North Wales marked the first onset of some hitherto unknown disease, the sudden stealthy attack of a nameless virus like the virus of the deadly Spanish influenza which swept lethally through the world just after the end of World War I, having developed itself prolongedly and in secret, somewhere – as experts later thought – in the basin of the Ganges.

Pete, elated by the emotional and physical fizz and anxious, no doubt, to show that the medical scientific corps of which he was a member was ready for anything and like the brave old British Territorials, willing to face the danger with a smile, pronounced all such ideas to be melodramatic and not based on factual reality; a mere hangover from earlier periods before medical science had got so comprehensive a grip on things as it now had. 'But,' said Mrs Buzbee, 'you can't say that nothing new and awful can ever suddenly happen. There has to be a first time, and when it's the first time you can't tell what's hit you until it hits you again, if you see what I mean.'

I recalled a couple of lines of verse I had several times used in my past career by way of valediction to pupils leaving the school. The lines had seemed to me very suitable at the time, though later I have doubted whether they were fully understood.

'One gazes,' I now said to Mrs Buzbee, 'down "a vista of horrible eventualities, past calculation to the end of time".'

'Quite so,' said Mr Buzbee.

'You take the very words out of my mouth,' said Mrs Buzbee.

'Sad,' said Pete.

'On the contrary,' said Irma. 'What's all this about a vista of things to come? How d'we know we aren't in the hell-fired vista already?'

'The whisky was good,' said Mr Buzbee, 'the wine's good and you have that lawn there, between the flowers and the sea.'

'Meantime,' said Irma, taking a big gulp of burgundy, 'we are surrounded by overcrowded slums described by the British as "congested areas" where pullulate semi-literate children without a future, having the privilege, if they can get that far without being run down by touring motorists, to gaze from time to time at such aspects of civilization as that bloody great house of Mrs Fitzpayne.'

'Bloody or not,' Pete said to me, 'I'm glad you reminded me. You were supposed to go call on her this afternoon, weren't you?'

I said that I was.

'Well, I met her on my way down here and she said to tell you that she had to be in town this afternoon anyway, so she'd look in here instead. All right?'

I said it was, but had to deal with a quick jab of resentment at the fact that Pete had, it seemed, so nearly forgotten a message of considerable importance to myself. That such had been the case with Pete was plain enough. 'Ogling oculist' was the phrase which jumped into my mind as I watched him examining Mrs Buzbee.

To what extent, I asked myself, is it permissible for a person to allow a sudden sexual obsession to drive matters of concern to other people out of his head?

I was seeking to formulate some way of posing this question in a generalized form when Pete looked at his watch and said he had to ' dash ' back to his office.

Once again he had underestimated the unsleeping Major Riddle. Major Riddle claimed he could read the Colonel like a book. He knew, intuitively, in advance, just what tricks the Colonel was likely to be up to under any given circumstances. By terribly daring and devious means he actually waylaid and sabotaged the medical officer's report on its way to higher authority. To clinch the matter, he took occasion to call upon the medical officer concerned and, relying upon his intuition, gave that officer to understand that he, Riddle, knew all. Any attempt by the medical officer to trace his original report or to manufacture a new one would bring the officer before a court martial. Terrified, the medical man reported to the Colonel. He passed on Major Riddle's parting remark. The Major had said, 'I just can't wait to see that son-of-a-bitch hopping through those minefields, while the machine-guns go bocka-bocka-bock.'

Just before this catastrophic happening, while the Colonel was still in a state of euphoria induced by belief in the efficacy of his phantom ulcer, he had carried a step further his preparations for life in a world free from war, hunger, oppression and fear. Without claiming to be able to peer very far into the future, Colonel Fitzpayne had decided that you could not go very wrong in acquiring, as a preliminary, and as a base of operations, a stately home somewhere in Britain. On a brief motor tour through the South and West country, he had espied on the lovely coast just west of our town a mansion which seemed to him likely to fill the bill.

It was a huge Palladian structure, designed, it is true, by an inferior architect but, although lacking elegance, impressive. Also, within its spacious confines it embraced large remnants of earlier architectural achievements, Carolean and Tudor, which could be held to enhance its historical interest and value.

From sometime in mid-nineteenth century until 1940, it had been the property of a rich, but abnormally nervous, British baronet and his wife. During the first bombings of London, this elderly couple had resided in the mansion, horri-

34

Four

'Just who,' asked Mr Buzbee, as we sat alone together on the lawn after lunch, 'is Mrs Fitzpayne?'

I could not imagine why he should be interested. Her name had only been mentioned twice in his presence, once when Irma had referred to her 'bloody great house' and then when Pete passed on her message to me. However, at the moment Mrs Fitzpayne was very much on my mind. Within an hour or so I had an appointment with her to discuss a matter of importance to myself and indeed to the whole of our community. Perhaps it might be beneficial to marshal for the benefit of a stranger, and objectively, the facts of what I classified as the Fitzpayne situation. So I set about summarizing for Buzbee a narration very familiar by then to me.

There are, one reads, adventurers seeking to marry rich widows. It must be considered a discredit to their group that none of them had as yet succeeded in sinking his hooks into Mrs Fitzpayne. She was, one would have supposed, a prize well worth extra effort. She was unusually rich. She had the figure of a civilized savage, the whole of it enclosed tautly in a skin having the sheen and texture of oiled silk. When she lightly swung her Edwardian umbrella her movement suggested an athlete swinging a baseball bat. When she pointed with it at features of the landscape, it might have been an

31

assegai by a well-knit old-time Zulu. She constituted a challenge which the adventurers apparently had been unable to meet.

She was the relic – if the technical term does not evoke a picture of passive resignation, in her case totally misleading – of George B. Fitzpayne, sometime Colonel in the United States Army. She spoke of him freely and often. Her references mingled some wonder, some awe, some pride. For the most part she spoke of him rather as a person might speak of an exotic animal, a cheetah, say, which at one time had had the run of the house in place of the more conventional dog. 'George,' she often said, 'was just the frankest, frankest man I have ever met.'

This frank personage was already a colonel and only a small distance on the bright side of middle age when she, half-American and half-English, being aged at the time eighteen, met and married him in London on the day after Christmas, 1943. By almost ceaseless vigilance and intrigue, Colonel Fitzpayne had risen to that rank without quitting the security and relative comfort of an army base camp in Louisiana.

I say 'almost ceaseless vigilance' because once he slipped up, with nearly lethal consequences.

Signing a leave-pass for himself, he had gone to New Orleans where he spent a fortnight very lavishly eating, drinking and whoring. During his absence he was viciously intrigued against by a certain Major Riddle, a man who seemed to have dedicated his life to discommoding, harrying, and, if possible, wrecking Colonel Fitzpayne. Shortly before leaving for New Orleans, Colonel Fitzpayne had taken what he believed were adequate measures to send the obnoxious Riddle to his death on some island in the Pacific. He had shown himself overconfident. On his return to the camp, he found that Riddle had put in his time so effectively that not only Riddle, but Colonel Fitzpayne also were posted to the European Theatre of Operations.

The Colonel thus arrived in England at a moment when D-Day, although its date was not yet fixed, already loomed, a

menace as sure as Fate. The Colonel seemed to have be fixed up as an integral part of the military machinery design to cross the Channel, drive the Germans off the Fren beaches, push them violently across France and over t Rhine.

The Colonel was a man quite able to think of two thing at once. He thought about the invasion of France. He con sidered plans for dealing with that eventual situation.

At the same time, since his non-survival would render a planning otiose, it was more practical to assume his surviva and to make preliminary arrangements for the life-after-wa and to take advantage of the Four Freedoms which the Allie Governments purposed to establish as the inalienable birth right of mankind.

He thought of money, he also thought of sex.

The consequences of his disastrous outing in New Orleans had convinced him that, at least for the time being, and in particular until he could extract the thorn of Major Riddle from his flesh, the prudent thing to do would be to have his sex life handily by him, carrying it about with him wher necessary, rather than have to take his eye off Major Riddl while he went foraging for it. On the occasion of his thir meeting with the future Mrs Fitzpayne he said to her wit that frankness which she reverently remembered long after hi death, 'Naturally I want to marry you. Every time I look you you give me a hell of a sexual jolt. And then you're damn rich.'

As the looming D-Day took more and more unmistakab definite shape, Colonel Fitzpayne for his part took measur which he considered nearly foolproof to ensure his surviva He intended to be partially incapacitated by a stomach ulc during the danger period. The necessary measures were e pensive. They also exposed him to the possibility of futu blackmail by a distinguished medical officer. X-ray phot graphs had to be purloined from the file of a genuine ulc sufferer and described as being those of the Colonel. On t basis of these photographs, a false report had to be written.

B

fied by the sufferings of the capital, but at the same time regarding them as being in the nature of a newsreel recording the violent misfortunes of other people elsewhere. Later in that year, the Germans from their bases in Northern France had taken to making bombing raids on the industrial areas of South Wales. Almost nightly they used to go humming over the mansion northwards towards and across the Bristol Channel, aiming for Cardiff, Swansea, and points adjacent. For some time the baronet and his lady continued to regard these events in the industrial belt to the North as taking place in another world. Then, within a single week, three German planes got into difficulties, two of them as they approached the south coast outward bound, the third as it returned from its mission. The first two were forced to jettison their bombs just as they crossed our section of the coast. The third, returning from its mission, suffered engine trouble, crashed noisily, and lit up the whole area with its flames.

The baronet hurried to the conclusion that for occult reasons the High Command of the German Air Force had placed our apparently innocuous town, contributing absolutely nothing to the war effort, on its map of targets to be attacked. He decided that the only way in which he and his wife could elude the malign ferocity of General Goering, was to make tracks as soon as possible for a small property they had in Cumberland. It was at first their intention simply to close up the mansion until the return of suitably normal times. But the loosing off of high explosives within half a mile of them, the blaze of flames signifying war, had disturbed their nerves and their judgement. These events had caused them to lose faith in the idea that normal life must return like the sun after night. It seemed to them suddenly that the world was erupting like a rogue volcano. It was possible that one might be able to climb out over the rim of the crater into Cumberland and cower there, hoping without much confidence that one would not be smothered and mummified by the lava.

In this mood they offered to sell the mansion to the local Council for a song.

They were apparently actuated too by a vague sense that to hand the place over at fearful financial sacrifice to some kind of public authority would be regarded somewhere, somehow, as a propitiatory gesture in the direction of what they dimly apprehended as the modern world.

The members of the Council, composed at that time of the senile and of *embusqués* on the make, accepted the offer. They, too, were affected by a kind of fatalism about the future. But in their case this fatalism was blithely optimistic. Even the relatively small sum of money demanded by the baronet was not immediately available to them, but under the influence of those bombs and those flames, they took the view that either everything was going to hell in a handcart, in which case budgetary details might as well be disregarded, or else things would pretty soon start looking up all round, and the necessary funds would appear from somewhere, perhaps from a Government keen as mustard on democracy and local initiative.

The baronet agreed to receive the payments on the instalment system. But by the early spring of 1944 it was disagreeably apparent to the members of the Council that no chiliastic world's end was immediately in sight. Still less did their mental money-diviners report the existence of magic reserves of cash or credit just under the barren surface of reality.

It was at this point that Colonel Fitzpayne made his appearance as a god from the powerful and luxurious machine put at his disposal by the United States Army. He soon wormed, or shook, out of the haggard Councillors the financial facts of their purchase from the baronet.

The Colonel spoke of comradeship in arms, of the heavy burdens and high endeavour which the British and the Americans shared in their pursuit of noble objectives. Taking, as he admitted afterwards, a bit of a chance, he mentioned with a small sob in his throat, that one of his forebears on his mother's side had been a passenger in the *Mayflower*. The English west country had thus been ever close to his heart. He was prepared, or rather Mrs Fitzpayne was prepared, to buy the mansion for a sum twenty per cent in excess of that still owing to the baronet, whose dunning letters from Cumberland had become more frequent and more threatening as he benefited from the physical security and total idleness of his life among the northern hills. The Council disclosed an obstacle. Under some new regulations, they were prohibited from reselling to a private individual what had become a piece of public property. The Colonel at first supposed that they had invented the regulation as a bargaining counter.

On being convinced that it really existed, he had a lawyer look into the matter. This investigation revealed that if the property were sold, not to a private individual, but for some public purpose, such a sale could be deemed not to fall within the provisions of the regulation. Still happily unaware of what had happened to his borrowed ulcer, Colonel Fitzpayne took further time off to arrange for the formation of a private company to be known as the Westward Ho! Trust. Of this organization eighty per cent of the shares were held by Colonel and Mrs Fitzpayne and the remainder allocated to a distant cousin of Mrs Fitzpayne who was right enough in the head to be able to sign his name, but not to take on anything more complicated in the way of business.

The Colonel then informed the Council that it was the purpose of the Westward Ho! Trust to purchase the mansion not as a private dwelling place, for this would obviously be out of keeping with the spirit and needs of the modern world. Rather, it was the aim of the Trust, as soon as the situation permitted, to transform the place into a school, designed to provide extraordinary amenities for the children of the town.

'It is our duty,' the Colonel said, 'to think of the younger generation. We may fall on the field of battle, but before we do so, we must see that the bright torch of our faith is passed undimmed into their hands.' Despite what the lawyer had said, two of the councillors held, or pretended to hold, that even these provisos would not enable them legally to dispose of the property. The Colonel rightly judged that this objection was raised not on behalf of the municipality as a whole, but in the interests of the two councillors concerned. Having arranged to make privately to these two agreed payments in cash, he was not surprised to learn that the council had voted unanimously in favour of the sale.

But this happy outcome was clouded by the news of Major Riddle's successful *coup* and increasingly visible signs that the dreadfully risky venture against the Continent could not now longer be delayed. The Colonel decided upon a stroke which combined audacity with shrewdness.

Pretending to have heard nothing of the confrontation between Major Riddle and the doctor, he adopted as quickly as could be done without arousing suspicion, a conciliatory, and after some time positively friendly attitude towards the Major. With a stiff upper lip and an air of calm, which nevertheless gave evidence of deep emotion within, he spoke of the future; of the hazards of a soldier's life; of the probability that from this venture, glorious as it was, he, the Colonel, might never return. As for his own life, he was perfectly prepared to lay it down in the course of his manifest duty. But he must think of his wife, of his children as yet unborn. (Not, in point of fact, so much as conceived.) He explained to the Major how, with these considerations in mind, he had bought this abiding place for his widow-to-be and future children in the gracious little earthly paradise of South Western England. But had he, he asked, acted impulsively? He most heartily wished for an outside opinion on the property he had purchased. Would the Major ever find the time to come with him on a short trip of inspection and appraisal?

The Major was not of course totally deceived. His instinct immediately told him that the Colonel was up to no good.

Five

But he reasoned, and this reasoning had results very unfortunate for himself, that now of all times was a time to keep
the Colonel under his closest surveillance. The desired objective, that is to say the sight of Colonel Fitzpayne hopping
across a mine-strewn beach while German machine-guns blazed
at him, seemed almost within reach. It would be a mortifying
disappointment to have the Colonel slip out of the net now.
He had no idea how Fitzpayne might manage so to slip, but
he was determined to keep him under his eye. He thought, too,
and here again his deductions were faulty, that the Colonel's
assumed eagerness to take him along on this trip to the West,
must be taken to mean that the Colonel was anxious not to
have him come at all. He went.

On earlier visits to his newly acquired property, the Colonel
had gained a clear idea of the layout. The huge house sat on a
moderately elevated plateau, from which, despite the architect's stylistic pretensions, it seemed to glower at the sea with
an air of sullen misgiving. It was approached by rather more
than a half-mile of avenue, rising steeply between a fairly
recent plantation of larches. At the top the avenue broadened
into a wide gravel driveway which passed in front of the house
and swept circularly around extensive ornamental flower beds
to rejoin the avenue. Beyond the driveway the ground with its

plantation fell away sharply.

As I recall, Mr Buzbee interrupted me at this moment to say,

'I think I can see what happened next.'

'You divine the Colonel's purpose?'

'You have clarified his character and the stresses to which he was subjected.'

The Colonel had somehow procured for the trip a powerful but quite unmilitary-looking convertible, of American make, naturally. In the left-hand driving seat he discoursed bravely and continuously to Major Riddle on such topics as the state of the war, man's duty to his dependants and the charms of old world England. He was still talking as he swung the car into the avenue and accelerated sharply. Near the top he shouted, 'There's the house!' The Major craned and peered. As he did so, the Colonel took the car fast across the gravel, past the pillared front door, swung it again round the further-most arc of the circle, and at a certain point drove it straight off the gravel down the slope and into the trees. Under his determined guidance the right-hand side of the car, with crash-ing violence, struck the third tree on the right, taking the im-pact expertly just behind the windscreen.

'A merciful death in its way,' said the Colonel later. 'The Major never knew what hit him.' Some two or three seconds before the blow struck, the Colonel, without loosening his hold on the steering wheel, had thrust his body backwards and up-wards. As the car careened from the shock, he hurled himself, or was in a position to be hurled, clear of the machine, but landed with brutal force against the foot of a tree on the left.

'Just my luck,' he said in hospital when Mrs Fitzpayne was allowed to visit him some forty-eight hours later, 'that I was wearing a crash helmet and a pretty heavily padded jacket. Amazing how fast a guy thinks when something like that suddenly happens. Right there in the air I ducked my head sideways and got an arm up to protect it.'

His forearm was badly smashed, and the bones of his shoulder. Three ribs were broken and he suffered concussion.

Even Mrs Fitzpayne when she referred to the incident seemed not entirely confident that the Colonel's own account of it had been marked by his customary frankness. She said to me once, reflectively, 'I suppose it wasn't just luck, it was presence of mind. That was it. Major Riddle had just as good a chance of getting clear as George had. A better one, really, if he'd just had the necessary presence of mind. After all, neither of them could have known any better than the other, how could they possibly, the car was going to behave that way, running off the gravel for no good reason?'

Short of positively admitting that ever since the destruction of his ulcer by Major Riddle, he had been brooding on and planning this dangerous, one might almost say, courageous act in his struggle for personal survival, the Colonel made no effort to conceal his satisfaction with the outcome, or to restrain his self-congratulations. 'Kind of two birds with one stone,' he had apparently said to her on one occasion. 'Except that one of them didn't get killed. Look at it how you like, you have to laugh. Riddle was worried sick, I wouldn't wonder, thinking about that not very nice little moment when he'd be jumping off the landing craft on to a minefield and whether he'd ever live to send a card home from even half-way to Paris, and then bingo! he gets his come-uppance in this secluded sector of south-western England.

'And me? You know he was aiming to get me blown up or shot up over there in France. And what, quite accidentally, happens? I get providentially thrown out of that car, saved by my own presence of mind. I get multiple injuries. I'm in the hospital there for two and a half months. While all those other fellows, with the exception of the Major, are advancing gallantly across those Normandy beaches, I'm tucked up, incapacitated but without much pain, and enjoying freedom from fear like the men said, in a nice hospital bed. My grandmother in Indiana would have seen the hand of Providence in it all.'

And a good many months later as he lounged in the sun-room specially carved out of the south side of the mansion, he remarked, 'Isn't it just great the way things have turned out? Here's the war all over in the ETO. Hitler surrenders, and I have my health back to the point where I am ready and willing to undertake full military duties.'

At that period Mrs Fitzpayne recalled, remembering him as I said, in a way a person might remember the behaviour of a cheetah, she used to sing aloud the words of a ribald song then popular in the United States Army and supposed to be a satire on staff officers fighting the last months of the war from headquarters in Paris.

'I spent V-Day on a bidet at the Astor.'

'That's what they used to sing,' said the Colonel. 'I did better than that. Spent the day in the hay with my sweetie. And with that son-of-a-bitch Riddle out of the way, there wasn't anybody arranging to do me out of my due need of decorations either. A man gets smashed up in the Argonne, or smashed up in England, he's still on service in the ETO isn't he? Entitled to due recognition of services rendered. In my case, a helluva long way beyond the line of duty.' This, it seems, he would repeat with deep chuckles of satisfaction.

Mrs Fitzpayne's comment on the entire episode was, to say the least, curious. 'It was all,' she used to say whenever she returned to the subject, 'very, very educative.'

Her education in the school of life with George continued in the American Zone of West Germany. When the Colonel had spoken of returning to military duty, he had intended that his return should be for a matter of a few months. But he was posted to West Germany. To quote a speech he made to some visiting Congressmen, reported in the army newspaper, from which Mrs Fitzpayne had preserved the cutting, the Colonel saw 'In the situation of this great but unhappy people, we are offered a great opportunity, if we will but reach out and grasp it with both hands. I am a simple soldier. I know nothing of politics or the business of politics. But as a simple soldier accustomed to obey, I know that Providence has ordered me into the front line of the struggle for the minds of men, for freedom and democracy, and I hereby pledge myself to do all that a soldier can do to lead this often misguided but yet great people out of the darkness of the past towards the bright lights of the future.'

Nobody seized the available opportunities with both hands more eagerly than the Colonel himself. One gathers that if he had had four hands they would all have been equally busy. No crock of gold seemed too heavy for him to lift, no pie too small for him to put a finger in. Taking only a few months to look around and settle down, he lodged himself in a key position. It was one which enabled him to sell as scrap whole fleets of new, or almost new, American Army vehicles, whole depots and hangars full of mechanical equipment. For his services the Colonel received between twenty-five and thirty per cent of the gigantic profits ultimately made by the dealers.

This was big money.

But the Colonel did not disdain other payments which, though relatively small, added up to very handsome sums. For as large a bribe as he judged the traffic would bear, he would take almost infinite pains to arrange for the provision of official de-Nazification papers to some badly harassed war criminal. Equally, for adequate payment, he would undermine, harry and denigrate in the eyes of the relevant American authorities, some self-styled representative of the new 'new Germany', who might be inclined to make himself unpleasant and even dangerous to war criminals and former leaders of the SS. Once or twice he was approached with offers of bribes to be given for services rendered, by representatives of the 'new men' themselves – Liberals, Socialists and the like.

But reluctant as he was to turn away any offer of money, the Colonel refused. He said to Mrs Fitzpayne, 'Those fellows may be all right, but somehow they don't just smell very good to me. Maybe if I knew more about politics I'd know just how far I could trust them. I'll do better just dealing with the fellows I can trust. You take an old SS commander, or a camp commandant and you can rely on him. He knows, and I know, that if he got even a little out of line with me, I could get him hanged in a fortnight.'

'George,' Mrs Fitzpayne would say, 'was never interested in politics. Nor am I.'

Mr Buzbee nodded at the end of his cigar. 'Such people,' he said, 'when it comes to bedrock essentials usually turn out more truly political than anybody else. So far as politics are concerned they are the original Heathen Chinee in the game.'

I had to admit to myself that this was indeed true of Mrs Fitzpayne. For what she meant by not being interested in politics was that she knew absolutely nothing, and cared less, about the political history, the political present, the constitution, or the programmes of the political parties, in any of the countries in which, since the death in the mid-1950s of George Fitzpayne, she had resided: or rather, alongside which she had moored herself ready to hack through the painter with a sharp cutlass at the first sign of officials with tax demands thundering down the quay.

By the standards of the late Colonel Fitzpayne, her education, conducted under his direct supervision, was complete.

Unlike millions of newspaper readers and television viewers exhausting themselves and sinking finally into numbed torpor after seeking to disentangle the complex skeins of national and international politics, and to interpret with at least a show of shrewdness, the acts and statements of political chiefs the world over, Mrs Fitzpayne refused to allow herself to be wearied or confused by such considerations. Broadly speaking, the two divisions of the world were marked by the division between the tax collectors or would-be tax collectors, and their victims or potential victims.

Coolly examined from this point of view, alleged differences between the Conservatives and Labour parties, the Republican and Democratic parties, Gaullists and their opponents, and statesmen on one side or the other of the Iron Curtain, seemed to be, at the best, insignificant. Stalin and Eisenhower, Macmillan and Khruschev, Harold Wilson, L. B. Johnson, not to mention Chairman Mao, Uncle Tom Cobley and all such predatory fauna, were all basically tax collectors. And most of those whom one heard raising the at-first encouraging cry 'Throw the rascals out' turned out to be ex-tax collectors seeking to get back on the job, or people who had not had a chance as yet to collect taxes but were anxious to try their hand. By the very law of their nature, the essential activity of all governments, whatever shifts of maquillage or even face-lifting they might adopt in order to differentiate their political complexions, consisted in riding roughshod, pig-headed and ruthless, over any potential tax payer who might be unlucky enough to be detected by them.

The potential tax payer lived in perpetual danger of being stripped to the skin and then flayed. Graduates of the Fitzpayne educational establishment had, however, learned to keep an eye open for the silver lining always providentially tacked on somewhere to even the darkest cloud. The silver lining, the spark of hope, the dram of eau de vie, which could save one from sinking into despair, consisted in the fact that, again by the law of their nature, all governments, all systems of tax collection, were rotten with corruption. While one must, of course, exploit to the full every legal and illegal trick of evasive action, the task, arduous but rewarding, of all those who wished not to fall victims but to survive, was to probe and to seek out every human avenue to this inner corruptibility and drive up it as far and as fast as it was possible to go.

'Your analysis is succinct,' said Mr Buzbee.

'Accurate, I believe,' I said.

'One point,' said Mr Buzbee, 'in this matter of the school. As I understand it, the Colonel originally bought the place only on the understanding that it was to be converted into a school for the benefit of the local and possibly other children. I take it this has never been done?'

'It has not,' I said.

'As a result,' asked Mr Buzbee, 'of what precise jiggery pokery?'

'The relevant document, that is to say, Colonel Fitzpayne's signed assurance to the Council, given early in 1945, has disappeared.'

'Filched by the Colonel or his agents? Or later by this relic of whom you speak?'

'It is not exactly known. In any case I think the point probably not germane to the central issue. I may say, however, that from certain indications I have received, I personally believe that Mrs Fitzpayne, anxious (as she would no doubt say) to carry out in letter and spirit the wishes of the departed, in fact arranged for the disappearance of that document.'

'But,' said Mr Buzbee.

'You are going to object,' I said, 'that in that case surely the original situation, that is to say the situation in which the Council was not legally empowered to sell the property at all, may be said to be reconstituted. We are back, you think, to square one. But if you will give the matter a moment's further thought you will reflect that at least in this country, nothing ever goes back to square one. Since the events of 1945, there have been changes of government, changes of policy, and whole libraries full of new and frequently contradictory regulations.'

'And your own interest in the matter?'

'Is both personal and impersonal. Intensive and extensive. Your judgement of it would depend on whether you proceed from the inside outwards, or from the outside inwards.'

'Obviously,' said Mr Buzbee, 'but,' he added, looking past me in the manner of Sherlock Holmes peering out of his window in Baker Street, 'here, if I am not mistaken, is our client, or rather the relic, now.'

Six

Swinging the baseball bat, poising the assegai, Mrs Fitzpayne came down the steps with Irma, who at the bottom
stood with her for a while laughing and exercising English,
then moved away to survey, and where necessary tend, the
lower reaches of the herbaceous border. With Mrs Fitzpayne
approaching our seat, there was a standing up, a brief introduction of Buzbee to Fitzpayne, Fitzpayne to Buzbee, talk
about how there was a lot of traffic on the road and it's
warmer today than yesterday, and then Buzbee said that he
really must excuse himself, he understood that the afternoon
post left at six o'clock and he had to get a letter in it.

Almost before he had stepped out of earshot, Mrs Fitzpayne
made an animal noise, something between a grunt and a snort.
Erupting suddenly out of that visage of a white female noble
savage, the effect of this brutish sound was always somewhat
startling. It could, I suppose, be judged as an act of candour.
It seemed designed to call attention to the animal nature of
mammals in general and of Mrs Fitzpayne in particular.

'Can't you just imagine,' Mrs Fitzpayne astoundingly said,
'who that letter's reporting to?'

I said I could not. I had not the faintest idea. I had only
just met Mr Buzbee that very morning.

'Buzbee, is it?' said Mrs Fitzpayne, 'I didn't catch it when

47

you introduced us. Who is he?' She snorted again and I thought of some lovely sleek pig down there in the Dordogne, rooting for truffles. I forgave her this intrusiveness, it was her nature. But I felt a warm loyalty to Buzbee, my friend of three hours' standing. I said, 'He and his wife are from Ireland. They are making a short stay in the hotel.'

'I mean, where have they just come from?'

'I told you, Ireland.'

'No they haven't. At least, he hasn't. I've seen him twice in town here, somewhere along in the last week, and once he was walking along the roadway just beyond the wall of our larch copse. He had on,' she added, 'a government-type hat. And just now as I came through the hotel I saw it hanging there in your lobby.'

I knew that if Mrs Fitzpayne had seen what she called a government-type hat anywhere she would automatically have mentally photographed the face under it. Years of experience, both before and after the death of Colonel Fitzpayne, had taught her that government-type men in government-type hats are all too often directly or indirectly connected with tax collection, agents direct or indirect of an oppressive régime. If she said she had seen Mr Buzbee, she certainly had.

I said, 'Probably somebody else in a similar hat.'

'Nonsense. I haven't made any mistake. He's not the kind of smudge-faced clerk they usually let loose, faces that you can't tell whether this one's the one you saw before or a new one. But this Buzbee's face, that's the kind where it's "once seen make a note of", like the man said.'

This further evidence, which I did not doubt, of something just a little enigmatical about Mr Buzbee was agreeable to me, like a little more garlic in the stew.

Mrs Fitzpayne brooded, obviously on the subject of Buzbee and then equally obviously turned that subject out of her mind in order to make room for a new one. 'I dropped by,' she said, 'to save you the trouble of trekking out to the house. I mean if you want an answer to your question. It wouldn't have been worth your while. The answer's still "no".'

The question she referred to was one of the highest importance. Looking at the entire matter as coolly as possible I could not avoid the conclusion that the answer must produce profound effects upon the whole of our community, plus incalculable repercussions in other spheres. My plan or scheme, in the implementation of which this was a first step, was complex. So complex, indeed, that at that time I carried about with me in my breast pocket, available for consultation at all times, a rough précis, covering the main points. I did so because late one night after a long walk through the streets of our town, and an hour or so of intensive brooding in my office, I had envisaged the whole enterprise with the utmost clarity. But in the morning a frightening thing had happened. Numerous essential features of the plan as I had viewed it the previous night now had simply faded from my mind. And in the absence of these, other aspects of it presented themselves in ugly caricature. They could be seen as naïve, inept, childish, grotesquely over-simplified.

For the greater part of that day I had nearly despaired. Then it had occurred to me that by exactly reproducing the conditions of the previous evening, I might recapture the clear picture I had then had. I repeated my walk through the town; I recalled, as exactly as I could, the number of drinks I had offered myself during the period of intensive brooding, and the precise length, in time, of this period.

The experiment was successful. But I had, as I say, had a fright. I was determined that the same thing should not occur again. Before going to bed I wrote my précis.

Now, under the shock of Mrs Fitzpayne's 'The answer is still no' I felt the need briefly to consult the document. Also it seemed important to emphasize the gravity of what she had said. I therefore said, 'This is something of a shock. Give me a couple of minutes to think it over,' and with that paced away from her to the far end of the lawn where the bank concealed me.

Perusal of the document re-clarified my ideas and gave me increased confidence. It was both succinct and stimulating.

In the interests of clarity, I had arranged it under various headings thus:

'General Over-All Objective: The benefit and uplifting of the human race.

'Immediate Objective: Benefit and uplifting of the people of the town in which I live.

'Motivation: Misery in which many people of this town – notably the children, the homeless and the old – now exist.

'Considerations to be discarded: Apparent smallness of project, possibility that other means more effective. These but alibis, excuses for non-action. Resoluteness required here.

'Means of immediate action: Persuasion of Mrs Fitzpayne to sell house to town at price so low that Town Council will not dare refuse to put up the money. House to be sold on condition it used as school premises, old age home, etc. All amenities.

'Means of persuading Mrs Fitzpayne to this course of action: Various means to be considered.

'(a) Appeal to decent humane instincts, with statistics showing condition of, in particular, children. Stress danger future human race. Delinquency, gangsterism, etc. etc. etc.

'(b) Warning of things to come. Probability general uprising British poor v. rich. Awkward position of semi-Americans. Unlikelihood Government capable effective restraint. Quit while quitting good etc. etc.

'(c) Sexual approach. Requires careful consideration. But not to be disregarded if all else fails. Potemkin etc.'

Over a period of five months and two weeks – that is to say ever since her return to our town from an extended tour of Egypt and the Indian sub-continent – I had made opportunities to talk with her at least once a week, discussing such issues as the rise in the crime rate, the progress of space travel, the life and times of the late Colonel. And, as our acquaintance ripened, I had taken occasion to draw her attention to the general situation of our community, viewed objectively, and in relation to the general trends of civilized life in the western world. And now it was just three days since I had raised the matter of my plan in precise form.

She had been less quick to grasp what was at issue than I expected. We had been sitting together on a sofa in her drawing-room. I had been forced to repeat myself.

In reply to her immediate outburst of 'Why the hell?' I had naturally begged her, like a Victorian suitor, seeking a lady's hand in marriage, not to give me an immediate answer, to examine the matter in all its aspects, to look deep into her heart and, of course, to consult Mr Groom. This Groom, who, to judge by an autographed picture she had, looked like a golf club secretary indicted for embezzling the club funds, was her guru or – if one chose to be offensive – her witch-doctor; in other words her personal tax accountant. This suggestion that she consult him was doubly unnecessary. It was so first because if she had any doubts about the matter at all she would certainly consult him in any case, secondly because the words were hardly out of my mouth when a maid interrupted us to say that Mr Groom was on the telephone. As we rose from the sofa in her drawing-room where we had been sitting, she had said to me 'It's no use your waiting. This conversation with Ashleigh' (Ashleigh was Mr Groom's given name) 'is going to be important. All my conversations with Ashleigh are important. When I talk to him, I talk for hours.'

The message conveyed to me via Pete Nordahl was the first communication I had had from her since that afternoon. And now here she was saying that it was not worth my while even to visit her and the answer to my question was 'no'.

I saw at once that a point of crisis had been reached. I thought of that tide in the affairs of men.

For weeks I had been keeping a card up my sleeve. It had become sufficiently apparent that were I to make sexual advances to Mrs Fitzpayne, this almost ostentatiously lusty widow was likely to respond, if not with an immediate acceptance at the drop of a hat, at least with some buzz and quiver at the nerve centres which might have a favourable effect on her judgement of the plan which was my real objective. Standing with her there on the lawn beside the pool, it occurred to me that I had possibly left the playing of this card a little late. She had already said 'no' and so saying had jabbed a hole in the lawn with the point of that up-to-the-minute umbrella, which now resembled in my eyes the sword of an extraordinarily well-developed knight plunged into the body of a dragon. The dragon, representing my plan, lay expiring in ludicrous defeat. I would not have been surprised to see her raise her foot and plant it symbolically on my plan, trampling it viciously.

This assessment of the position I instantly rejected as defeatist. It was by no means too late to play my card. Might it not indeed, I asked myself, be the case that it was precisely my failure to play that card which had produced, through pique and frustration, her superficially uncompromising negative? What then were the pros and cons, the arguments for and against playing the card now? I mentally listed them, putting the cons first with the idea of giving them a good run for their money, and offsetting any subjective bias I might have in favour of immediate action:

Con (1) – she might for some barely guessable reason reject my sexual advances. Suppose, for instance, she was engaged in an adequately satisfactory affair with Groom? In that case my entire position would be disastrously weakened. I thought of Groom and his appearance and although I was still supposed at this stage to be giving full play to the Cons, I decided that this one was a non-starter.

Con (2) – she might be capable of, as it were, splitting her personality. She might, that is to say, satisfy her sexual appetite while at the same time refusing to allow this to colour her attitude to my plan, let alone to admit that this satisfaction in any possible way obligated her to look upon it more favourably. Such behaviour on her part could be regarded as amounting to a coolly barefaced swindle. Nevertheless it had to be seen as a possibility.

Con (3) – a variation of (2) above. In the first heady, enjoyment of this hypothetical sexual relationship, she might be sufficiently lulled by the pleasure of it to imagine, even to believe, that the plan was after all acceptable. Inevitably the technical arrangements connected with the handing over of the house and its spacious grounds would take time; months. And before the necessary papers could be signed, sealed and delivered, she might have become satiated.

Pro (1) – Suppose, for the sake of supposing, that she really was having an affair with witch-doctor Groom, the accountant, a meanly-shaped runt, if ever I saw one. By decisive action I should achieve two aims at once. I should forge sexual and emotional bonds between Mrs Fitzpayne and myself, and at the same time tend to destroy any similar influence exercised by Groom, which influence I felt sure would be employed in a manner inimical to the interests of my plan.

Pro (2) – Even in the unlikely event of a rejection, the declaration of my physical passion for her could surely not leave her unmoved. She would hardly be able to think of me and my plan without at least momentarily wondering whether after all an *affaire* might not have been at the worst fun, at the best delightful. In this state of mind she would be apt at least to postpone any final negative pronouncement on the subject of the plan.

Pro (3) – Assuming, as without undue optimism one was entitled to do, that at least during its early stages the *affaire* proceeded to her satisfaction, it might be by no means impossible to get the matter of the house and grounds informally sewn up so firmly that the completion of the legal technicalities could hardly be hindered without her being exposed to dishonour and ridicule.

She evidently interpreted my silence, which lasted several seconds, while I reviewed these elements of the situation, as the result of shock and disappointment on my part following the statement that the answer to my question was 'no'. Jabbing the sword into the dragon again, she said, 'Are you surprised at my answer?'

I said, 'Answer to what?'

'To your question.'

'What question?'

'Don't be a damned fool. Your question about the house.'

Looking passionately out to sea, I said, 'I am not being a damned fool. It's simply that there's another question in my mind which is really more important to me than the one I asked you.'

'What's that?'

I looked at her and, to put it coarsely (but I judged a certain brutal speed desirable) I let her have the passion from both barrels straight between the eyes, volubly.

She stiffened and then shuddered ever so slightly all over.

'Well, I'll be goddamned,' she said. 'Is that really so?'

I had already reloaded with fresh words and fired again. She then made a tiny grimace which served to assure me that I had been successful. Her head turned fractionally away from me before she checked the movement. But it was obvious to me that she had begun instinctively to turn her head to see whether Irma was, if not in earshot, at least watching us. She had checked the movement as unseemly.

I tactfully suggested that she might drive me up to her house where the interview could be continued in greater privacy.

She said, 'You're a fast worker.'

'That,' I said, vehemently, 'is nothing but an insult to yourself and me. Do you think I take you for a pushover? Don't you understand that I've felt this way about you ever since I set eyes on you?'

With a frankness which I recognized as a legacy of the Colonel, she said, 'Well, why the hell didn't you say so before?'

I said that my passion for her was such and meant so much to me, that for fear of a rebuff I had not dared put the matter to the test, postponing the crucial moment from week to week.

'Well,' she said, and began to walk across the lawn towards the steps leading up to the hotel. She was again unable to restrain herself from peering a little furtively sideways in search of Irma. But Irma was already invisible, engaged in her unceasing creative tasks among the flowering shrubs at the far end of the herbaceous border.

On the pretext that I feared I had left a drawer with important documents in it unlocked, I asked Mrs Fitzpayne to go ahead to the car while I went into my office to make sure. In reality I felt the need of a moment's breathing space between the mental exertions of the last quarter of an hour and the physical exertions, however pleasurable, scheduled for the immediate future. Above all I felt I needed the combined stimulant and nerve soothing effect of a half-glass of whisky. I recalled with satisfaction that Mrs Fitzpayne herself was a regular whisky drinker, had certainly drunk spirits of some kind since lunch and would therefore not be discommoded in the way poor Pete had been that morning.

Except for the low moan of the engine, we drove in silence through the town, out along the road between hillside and sea, and up the avenue to the mansion. As she always did when she stood on her own broad front doorstep, looking out across the gravel driveway, Mrs Fitzpayne remained for a moment looking with evident reverence towards the spot where Major Riddle had, as she sometimes put it, quoting Colonel Fitzpayne, 'made his rendezvous with death'.

'To think,' she said on this occasion, 'that if it hadn't been for his presence of mind, George would have gone out along with him. You certainly can see the hand of providence in it all.'

She led me, not to the big drawing-room where we normally conversed, but to a smaller room on the first floor which, she told me, had been the Colonel's smoking-room and 'Library'.

The handsome glazed bookcases were, so far as I could see through the glass, sparsely occupied by books. Noting my glance at the shelves she said, 'George always said he had too great a respect for books to have a lot of them about, which he was never going to have time to read.'

By way of what seemed to me a touchingly graceful indication, that despite the superficial formality of our earlier relationship she had in fact been warmly interested in my personal habits and preferences, she reached into a drink cabinet and without questioning me brought out a decanter of whisky and poured it for both of us. It was a signal of intimacy. For on earlier occasions she had always observed the convention of asking me what I wanted to drink.

Seeming suddenly younger than her age, she stood face to face with me, said ' Here's to us ', knocked back her drink in a single gulp, watched me do the same with mine, and took the two steps forward which were necessary before we could embrace.

Seven

So far so very good. It was a relief to surrender myself to emotional and physical pleasure without need to bother for the moment about planning. I started to lead her to the wide couch, upon which the Colonel, presumably, once intently read a book or two and mentally organized the bringing down of Major Riddle. But she said,

'George used to say he liked me near him when he was reading or thinking. He didn't like to read or think for very long at a stretch. He said he wanted to have me available at all times. That's why the bedroom is right here next door. Let's go.'

As she said these last words her voice changed, perhaps to the voice she had had before she ever met the Colonel. She pushed upon the communicating door, but as she did so the silence of the spacious room beyond was pierced by a mechanical screech.

'Oh God,' she cried. 'It's the damned intercom. It'll be the butler saying somebody's come to call or somebody's telephoning, more likely.'

She unhooked the intercom instrument and listened to the distorted voice of, I suppose, the butler.

'Just a minute, just a minute while I think,' she told him. Turning to me she said tensely, 'It's Ashleigh. He wants to talk with me.'

'But,' I said.

She stood for a moment visibly wavering, torn by an internal struggle. Then with what I had to acknowledge was an admirable effort of will, a triumph, one might say, of mind over matter, she spoke into the intercom saying, 'All right. Put him through,' and exchanged the intercom for the outside telephone. While she waited for the butler to relay the call to this extension, she said, 'This is important. Very important.' I have to admit that I was stabbed by a spasm as sharp as gout, of simple jealousy and frustration. I even wondered whether my earlier surmise about her possible relations with the man Groom had not been correct after all. She said – gloomily, I was glad to note – 'We may have to talk for an hour.'

'But why,' I said, 'why now?'

She said, 'He's the best tax accountant in the business.'

Into the telephone she said, 'Hello Ashleigh, just a minute while I get settled.' She seated herself on the wide bed, beside a low table on which a note pad and pen lay ready. She looked up at me briefly, seeming for a moment to hesitate. But it was almost immediately clear from her expression that she had realized as plainly as I did that it would really be impossible for me at this stage to sit on the bed waiting or to wander into the next room and occupy myself for an hour or so with the remnants of Colonel Fitzpayne's library.

A wild thought crossed my mind that I might fill in the time by slowly undressing. Perhaps had this been winter time and I had been wearing a sweater over my shirt and perhaps if it were really cold a vest under it, such a proceeding might have presented itself as feasible. But here we were at the end of May with the weather more than usually clement. Even by dragging the proceeding out to the utmost, infringing every law of efficient use of time and motion, the whole action could not possibly take more than seven or eight minutes, after which I should be in the absurd position of lying there stripped, so to speak, for action, with no action possible except that of listening to Ashleigh Groom's thin voice whining urgently down the telephone, and her equally urgent responses. As I turned to the door she put her hand over the transmitter and said two words which sounded like *Ah Demang*.

I was already crossing the 'Library' before I realized the use of a couple of words of what she believed to be French was an effort on her part to romanticize a situation which might well have been regarded as sordid. The very inadequacy of the effort struck me as having the quality of pathos.

Having regard to the amount of whisky I had drunk during the afternoon, I thought it would probably be beneficial to my health to take a strenuously sweaty route back to town involving a walk of about three miles. It started with a rough plunge down from the driveway through the steep larch copse from which I emerged on a still unfrequented, poorly surfaced road meandering beautifully beside the sea. Things, I said to myself, as I pleasurably sniffed the sharp stink of salt and oil drifting in from the slick vomited up by that monstrous tanker and still invisibly hanging about in the offing, were conspiring together for good. In this cheerful mood I rounded one of the many bends in the road as it followed the indented coast, and realized that a short distance ahead of me on the inland side of the road was a bungalow known to the gossips of our town as 'Harrogate's Harem'.

It was inhabited by the secretary (Eileen) of Harry Harrogate, who was not the Chairman but incontestibly the most powerful member of the Town Council. Gossips are often malicious and often wrong. But in the case of Harry Harrogate and Eileen there seemed no room for doubt that they were right. The malicious pleasure occasioned by this relationship was evoked by the fact that although Harrogate himself wished, and perhaps even believed, that it could be kept secret, the ambitious Eileen was evidently of the opinion that to flaunt it, to nail, as it were, her colours to his mast, would ultimately prove to be an advancement of her personal interest.

Harry Harrogate himself was perfectly aware that this tiny scandal brought him into ridicule and some contempt among

the voting population, which was the only section of the population to whose opinion he attached the slightest value. The
ridicule and contempt were aroused not, obviously, by the fact
that this Councillor, married to a woman who amply represented in the flesh everyone's mental picture of what is meant
by a harridan, should be, as they said, 'getting a little something on the side'. It was rather by their appreciation of the
reasons for Harrogate's particular choice. The 'little something' was not physically more attractive than a hundred other
young women in the town, or a thousand of them if you went
a little further afield. And the gossips could name at least a
score of other young women who, judged on any system of
points you chose, could give Eileen cards and spades. Therefore, they pointed out, her principal attraction for Harrogate
must consist in the fact that she was his paid secretary who
could be fired if she failed to meet his demands. From this it
was a short step to the deduction that Harrogate, for all his
pretensions to physical charm, his all too visible desire to represent himself as a ladykiller, only restrained from entrancing
half the girls in the district on account of his selfless preoccu-
pation with public business, in reality lacked the sexual
steam to secure as his paramour anyone not on his pay-
roll.

I immediately noted with elation that, at this hour, on this
afternoon, Harrogate's car was parked in front of the bungalow, and that between the car and the front gate of the bungalow's tiny garden, Harrogate and Eileen were in what was
obviously the act of saying good-bye. Their attitudes were
characteristic. Eileen, seemingly oblivious of any observer,
had one skinny arm around his shoulder, and was gazing from
short range into his eyes with the expression of a spaniel em-
phasizing to its departing master that its emotions combined
passionate and even supine submission, with a fierce possessive-
ness which, if thwarted or disappointed, could earn him a sharp
bite.

Harrogate's attitude on the other hand suggested that of
the secretary of some teetotal association nipping out of the

side door of a public house and anxious to cut short the land-lord's jolly farewells before some keen-eyed member of the association can appear on the illicit scene. His ears alert as those of some stealthy feline to the approach of danger, de-tected even at that distance the sound of my footfalls upon the road. With a remarkably nervous lack of gallantry, he disen-gaged himself from Eileen, gave her what he evidently sup-posed might do as a formal gesture of employer to employee, and stepped briskly towards his car. I could see that he hoped to pretend that he had not noted my approach and to drive off before I could get near enough to accost him. I therefore raised my voice in a loud hallo. He stopped and looked in my direction with simulated surprise. Assuming a false smile, which in fact merely emphasized his exasperation, he waited rigidly and as I drew nearer said, 'Ah! It's the Paki-stani.'

This was an allusion, at once bitter and ostensibly jocular, to the fact that a year or so before I had tried to get the Town Council to intervene on behalf of a Pakistani family threatened on account of their origins with eviction.

Inspecting Harrogate, I experienced not for the first time, a sense of nearly eerie wonderment at the apparently impro-bable but still undeniable fact that the odds were not more than about 6-1 against this specimen proceeding in the dreadful course of time to the back benches of the House of Commons, and thence, if one dared to face the probabilities realistically, to the front bench and membership of our govern-ment. Every repulsive detail of his appearance and known character instead of reassuring one that such an eventuality was out of the question, confirmed to any cool student of affairs that the possibility of such a development could not be ruled out, let alone laughed off. The fellow, I had to admit to my-self, was what is called a 'natural' for political advancement.

His face, as Irma had justly remarked, resembled the blown-up photograph of a second-rate film actor which had been spotted with rain and then over-quickly dried in front of a fire. Sprouting from, although it looked more as if it were glued to, this visage, was a moustache which when turned up at the ends brought vividly to my mind a television picture I had once seen of the painter Salvador Dali. But it was as though halfway through the growing season the painter Dali had lost the courage of his own convictions and arrested the sprouting hair so that the upturned portions appeared not so much an arrogant assertion of something or other, as an aspiring squeak designed to attract attention without committing the owner of their subsoil to anything irrevocable. This truncated moustache was keeping all the options open. It was so meanly malleable that whereas, when its owner was moving around and about in his lady-killer persona, it turned roguishly upwards, but on the much more frequent occasions when he was the good-hearted but hard-headed man about politics, those points could be pulled down with a shrewd tug so as to form a strong straight horizontal line, intended simultaneously to distinguish this face from the majority of clean-shaven faces, while quietly asserting that this was not a face likely to countenance any form of eccentricity or nonsense.

I noticed that he was actually pulling down those points to the horizontal, or public purpose, position as I came up to him. I had studied this man sufficiently to speculate now with interest as to the particular accent and intonation in which he would choose to conduct the opening sentences of our conversation. So far as was possible for so brief an utterance, his first hail, greeting me as the ' Pakistani ' had been given in an unmistakably West Country brogue. Here, one felt, was a man who would have been apt to give at the town concert a rendering of ' Oop from Zummerzet,' while locals, yokels and tourists cheered. With his unfailing flair for the movement of public opinion, Harrogate had long since decided that the Zummerzet ploy was so old hat as to be potentially ludicrous. For more general purposes he employed a kind of *lingua franca* featuring a flatly indefinable accent and general intonation, just perceptibly flavoured with such burrs and honest grunts as might be calculated to set Drake's Drum beating faintly in the hearts of the listeners.

By way of keeping the fellow on the defensive, I looked ostentatiously at my wrist watch. Since the time was barely four o'clock of a week-day afternoon, this gesture would serve to remind him that any attempt to mutter nonchalantly that he had just given Eileen a run back from the office after the close of a tiring day, was foredoomed. He understood my movement and his lip, as though caught by some invisible hook, lifted in an involuntary snarl. I immediately regretted what I now saw to have been a foolish self-indulgence on my part. It was not part of my plan, it was indeed inimical to my plans in general, positively to aggravate the natural and inevitable hostility to myself of this flabby but venomous reptile. On the contrary, it was desirable to placate, appease and flatter him to whatever extent possible without humiliating self-abasement and abandonment of principles. After bowing to Eileen with just the right brand of familiarity and formality, I said to Harrogate, 'Well, I certainly am in luck. At least I am if you're going to town and would be kind enough to give me a lift.'

Seeking to match me with a hideous pretence at jocularity, he said, 'Sure you wouldn't care to do a bit of walking and get some weight off?' To this I replied, 'Harry, old boy, I've given up trying to look as fit for my age as you do for yours.' Since the man was physically negligible and a long way from being any sort of an advertisement for the health-giving properties of our local sunshine and sea breezes, I wondered whether perhaps I had in this gone a little too far. Fortunately it is nearly impossible to over-estimate the vanity of politicians and Harrogate accepted my remark with a smirk. 'All right,' he said, 'I'll come to the aid of your tottering footsteps. Get in, lad, get in.'

Settling myself beside him, I remarked first that it was a grand day, secondly that I had just come from paying a call on Mrs Fitzpayne.

'Look,' he said, 'if you are going to talk to me again about that matter of the Fitzpayne property, for God's sake forget it. The shot's not on the board.'

Eight

'I tried,' said Harrogate, 'to the best of my ability to make that clear to you at the outset. It never was on the board. And now with what we've had to spend in the public interest to face up to the very real oil menace, and I don't mind telling you very frankly that we've had to dip a bit deeper into the till than we dare to tell the ratepayers yet, we certainly are not in a position to start pouring out money on what, if you don't mind my saying so, is a pretty starry-eyed, hare-brained type of a scheme, which I don't mind saying I don't think the ratepayers would stand for and which I, as a humble member of the ratepaying fraternity, sympathize with their attitude in relation to.'

'But,' I said.

'Just a minute,' he said. 'Just let me have my little say. Then I'll listen to you till the cows come home, although you'll appreciate I'm a pretty busy man. What you have to appreciate is that this is a matter which involves the entire relationship between what I call the public sector and the private sector. If you follow my line of thinking, and I may say that it's pretty generally accepted as sound in quarters which you and I would probably not be inclined to quarrel with the judgement of, people I mean who deal with these things from positions of authority and expert inside knowledge, the public and private sectors are both complementary and, I want you to understand this, separate. Now you won't deny that this Fitzpayne property you're interested in falls very, very definitely into the private sector. And what you want is for the public sector to undertake certain responsibilities, certain criterions in relation to, coming down to brass tacks, this property. You must appreciate, in other words, you must be cognizant of, the implications of the situation which I have reference to. Public sector on the one hand, private sector on the other. See what I mean?'

I allowed this stream of verbal sewage to trickle past my ears as we approached the town, driving faster than Harrogate was accustomed to do for the sufficient reason that he preferred the risk of bashing a pedestrian to that of running out of words before he could decently dump me.

'My idea is,' I said, 'that the children . . .'

He broke in like a commercial breaking into a television programme. 'I know, I know,' he said. 'But aren't we getting just a wee bit sentimental?'

Closing my eyes as a futile protection against his noise, I daydreamed that I had been endowed with superhuman powers and could leap from my seat, balance myself like an avenging angel upon the boot of his car and from this position pour sugar and oil ruinously into his petrol tank.

'I think, if I may say so,' he said, 'we all of us need to clear our minds of what I sometimes call " emotive " conceptions. Nobody could accuse me of not having the interests of the young people at heart. At the same time, and I very, very definitely do not want to get pompous about this, I do happen to be a responsible elected representative of the people of this community. I have to hold the balance between one interest, perfectly justifiable mind you, and another, weigh things up according to the realities of the situation as I see it, and let me tell you that a lot of the things I have to do aren't the easiest things to do, not by a long chalk, meaning that if I let my heart guide my head, I'd probably be stumping the town for some project or other which I can see, just as well as you can,

C

would be desirable if it were realistic, but which that little bit of realistic appreciation I've picked up along a path which hasn't always been roses all the way, tells me simply isn't consonant with the realistic factors in the given situation as we have it.'

'Just so,' I said.

He took a hand off the wheel and used it to slap me on the thigh. 'Of course I'm not convincing you, you old star-eyes. But changing the subject before the row starts, as the old tale says, I've got a bit of info which should be genuine grist to the mill of a man like you with ideas for this community of ours. Shall I tell you something?'

'Do,' I said.

'Well now, listen. Tomorrow at approximately this time, your humble servant is going to be interviewed by a television team. I won't say it didn't take a little bit of the old savvy to pull this one off, but leaving that aside, which is simply a matter of personal satisfaction to myself, I think I can say that this television interview is going to do at least as much that will be beneficial to this town which we all of us mutually love, as anything which anyone can dream up in relation to the future, immediate or distant. Get me?'

'Magnificent. Terrific. What will you talk about?'

'The way I see it, I'm going to talk first, foremost but not, don't get me wrong, all the time about the fight which this town put up and definitely waged against the menace of oil pollution along our coast. It's concrete, it's dramatic, by which I mean to say it has the quality of great drama. Great television, if you see what I mean. The point about television as I see it, is that you can act the thing out in a way that brings the nub of things bang home to the general public, in a way that columns of words can't do. Just for instance, I have it worked out how I'm going, at a critical moment, it's a sort of gimmick, if you like, but it's going to be damned effective, I'm going to take off my coat to show the way, don't you see, that we took our coats off to the problem, and I'm going to roll up my sleeves, get the idea? It's going to be a mauve shirt the sleeves I'm rolling up of, and don't laugh about that because it isn't I'm turning queer, it's just that I happen to have the word from the telly people that mauve's just the colour they want you to have for the telly. A white shirts kills the face, it seems, and a shirt that's what they call too strongly patterned distracts attention from the person in question. And what I always say is if the technicians want something, we should recognize that they probably know what they want and we should play along with them, within, of course, reasonable limits.'

'So you roll up your sleeves.'

'You see the way that punches home the message? And not just this particular message, about oil and so on, but the message, and I don't want to be even a little bit pompous about this, the message we have to bring home to the whole of this country, how we have to roll up our sleeves and get cracking. See what I mean?'

'That will be,' I said, 'an item worth seeing. When will it be screened?'

'I don't know exactly. It's not going out what they call "live", you know. But here's something I'd like to do for you. This thing's taking place, being filmed I mean, in the small Council chamber in the Town Hall. There won't be room for many of the general public and I don't want to be talking to a big local audience. But I'd be very happy to extend to you and your lady wife and Mr Nordahl, if he'd care to come, an invitation to be present along with a number of my colleagues of the Town Council and other leading personalities and so on and so forth.'

I said that I should be delighted, and was sure that Irma and Pete would be delighted likewise.

On the following afternoon I arrived a little early at the Town Hall. Pete had declined the invitation on the ground that he was busy, although, as I quickly ascertained, his business consisted in taking Mrs Buzbee for a sightseeing trip along the coast. Irma and Mr Buzbee were to join me in the Town Hall after going with Farragut, to lend him moral support while he attempted to extract some tools which he claimed belonged to him, from his former employer. This was the proprietor of a garage and motor car repair shop about equidistant between our hotel and the Town Hall. Farragut's employment there had lasted no more than a fortnight. As I have said, he had been accused of time wasting and pilfering. The most specific charges were that he had used the time and materials of the garage to construct various small electrically operated gadgets which he then proposed to smuggle out and sell to anyone who wanted, for instance, a cigarette lighter which would simultaneously light a cigarette and project an electric beam of light across the room, or a device for amplifying the voices of people on the telephone.

His employer also brought the vague charge that Farragut 'made a pigsty' of every place he entered. By this he seems to have meant that when packing cases with, for example, spare parts were delivered at the garage, it was Farragut's practice to tear them open with whatever lever or other instrument came to hand and after taking out the contents, leave the floor strewn with the broken packing case and the straw, kapok, or other material in which the parts had been packed. The garage proprietor said that employing Farragut meant that he would have to employ someone else to clean up after him.

A glance round the Council chamber at the Town Hall, which I had never entered before, was sufficient to expose as characteristically fraudulent Harrogate's pretence that we were going to be among a very small number of highly privileged guests; comically so, I thought, since anyone invited on that basis could discover immediately on arrival that there was room for virtually everyone in town whom Harrogate was likely to regard as being worth so much as a nod or even a greasy smile.

At first sight the Council chamber seemed to be full of men in mauve shirts. They were all, of course, Harry Harrogate, who twitched about the place like a dragonfly with an itch, mending a political fence here, licking a boot there, and over there giving some humble admirer a rewarding eyeful of the hero about to be pictured for the subsequent inspiration of millions. He asked me twice where Pete Nordahl was and I told him that so far as I knew, Pete had been delayed by an urgent consultation. A question of a tourist driving his family through town when their young and beautiful daughter was inexplicably stricken with total blindness in the left eye. They had enquired for the leading oculist in the town, had been directed to Pete.

What could he do? Desolated as he was at the prospect of missing the Harrogate television filming, he had his duty not only to traditions of medical science, but to the town itself which couldn't otherwise than benefit from this proof that, in addition to its other amenities, it had a skilled oculist ready to succour any stricken visitor. This highly-coloured lie was accepted by Harrogate as a full explanation of Pete Nordahl's absence, for the reason, I suppose, that Harrogate was incapable of supposing that anything short of some sensational and unlikely happening could account for anyone foregoing the privilege of accepting his invitation to see him in his mauve shirt in front of the TV cameras.

'Well, just so long as he got the invitation.'

And I realized that the only reason why I and Irma had been asked was because Harrogate considered it important to invite Pete. This was to the good. Pete had not yet stood for election to the Council, and in fact I doubted whether he was very likely to do so. But through his extensive professional connections he was certainly influential, or capable of exercising influence, behind the scenes. And Harrogate could not imagine that such a man would not sooner or later seek to extend and exploit such influence by entering politics. To this extent, therefore, Harrogate felt impelled to suck, as schoolboys used to say, up to him. It was a fact which I noted as being possibly of future use in the furtherance of my own objectives.

As I talked with Harrogate, the television technicians were already moving about with their air of dedicated aloofness, laying cables and shifting tripods. Just behind me one of them cursed coldly and violently as though some outsider had blundered clumsily into the laboratory where scientific high priests were getting ready to split the atom. Turning, I saw that Farragut, advancing shakily on his bandy legs, had tripped over a cable and nearly brought to the ground the piece of apparatus to which it was attached. Joining Harrogate and myself, he addressed us out of the corner of his twisted mouth, swivelling his eyes sideways to survey the room, as though in fear that policemen or stewards might be lurking to apprehend him. He was certainly in a state of agitation, his tone and words seeming to indicate that he feared he might once again be held responsible for something or other.

'You'll excuse the interruption,' he said. 'But I thought I'd better just slip along and report. No fault of mine,' I clearly heard him say, 'but you get these kids playing Buddha and what the hell can anyone do?'

Harrogate tapped with his feet and flexed his muscles inside the light fawn-coloured suit, which made him look like a mysteriously animated dummy inside a suit in the window of a cheap tailor. He kept switching his attention from Farragut to the technical preparations for the filming, as though he too like the technicians, was afraid that a vast enterprise was going to be interfered with by trivial incursions from the outside world.

'What? What, what, what's all this?'

His brusque manner heightened Farragut's state of agitated defensiveness.

'Covered with oil from the beach they were,' Farragut was heard to state. 'Though I bet if they'd been told once they'd been told twenty times not to go playing on that stinking sand on the far beach.'

Harrogate gave him his full attention and glared. 'What the hell are you talking about?' he demanded in a furious mutter. 'There's no oil on that beach and everyone knows it.'

Farragut repeated that there they were dancing around like black imps and one of them said, 'Let's play Buddhist priests.'

70

Farragut said that kids that age shouldn't be allowed to read the newspapers.

'What's this in aid of?' said Harrogate belligerently.

Nine

Farragut could be seen to be outraged. Here he was with a great sense of duty done, yet rewarded not with ha'pence but with kicks. He actually managed to bring his furtively wandering gaze round until he was for a moment looking Harrogate in the eye. He might have been facing a trainer who had interrupted his attempted explanation of some nasty business on the rails.

'If you'd just let me make my report in accordance with the facts of the matter,' Farragut said. '"Let's play Buddhist priests," was what these two black-looking imps said, and one of them said, "That oil stuff won't burn, you know that," and the other said, being at the moment just at the entrance to the garage, "there's a petrol can here with a screwtop loose and I'll pour it over us." Mrs Ballantyne and Mrs Buzbee were a step or two behind me,' Farragut said, 'and I don't think they were paying much attention, but I just happened to hear the remarks passed between these two kids and I thought it was just a game. Well, I mean, can you blame me?' I hardly knew how many times Farragut asked that. 'Just a game was what I thought and then we'd just passed by the garage yard to go to the shop entrance looking for the boss man to make this enquiry after my tools I was enquiring after, when God Almighty we heard a shriek and dammit if there weren't those two kids screaming and running way up the yard with little flames flaming out of them, flames of fire.' He was jumping about with gestures by now. ' Mind you, and that's what I said to myself right away, they can't have poured more than a trickle or so of petrol out of that can, or they'd have gone up like flaming torches. They were running straight for that back part of the garage where there were God knows how many cars parked, some of them half stripped down for repairs, and those cars are standing in pools of petrol and grease that you could go into it over the top of your shoes, and piles of shavings and straw and God knows what that I swear nobody's cleaned up since I left the place, and why the man wants to keep his place in that condition, a danger to the public, I'm sure I don't know. So Mr Buzbee and your missus they start running after the kids to shout to them, seeing the horrible danger. But it looked to me as though the kids were going to get into that mess of cars and petrol and junk and all that before those two catch up with them. And if that happens, I said to myself, there'll be little short of a holocaust. They were putting themselves right in danger of a holocaust. So what I did, I ducked back into the shop and I grabbed the telephone and I telephoned the fire brigade and I told them to get out there pronto. And then I came on here to report on the matter.'

For just a second I was too shocked and dazed to take in what Farragut had said. Then I grabbed and shook him.

'But the others,' I said, 'what happened to them?'

'Take it easy, mister,' Farragut said. 'After I'd taken all due steps to notify the fire brigade I turned this way out of the shop, there wasn't any point in going messing around at the garage at that stage of the game, and I came off here to report as seemed the thing to do.'

I left him still talking as I stumbled across the cable and out of the Council chamber. Twice I lost my way in the musty corridors of the Town Hall, and by the time I got to the steps I was shaking so I nearly fell down them. In the street I started shouting ' Irma!' although the garage was hundreds of yards away. I went pounding along the pavement, and staggering round the corner I saw standing at the entrance to the garage, a ragged, bedraggled looking, hardly recognizable quartet composed of people of very uneven height. My heart was beating so thunderously that I seemed to have difficulty even in registering that Irma was after all alive.

One of the small children jerked my attention towards itself with a howl. Trying to grasp what was specially peculiar about the child, I noted with shock that it was a small girl with a mop of bright hair hanging down on one side of her face and thick on top, but with the other side of the head seemingly almost bald as though shaven. Not shaven, I said to myself, singed. I stood staring at that fuzz or stubble, not only because it was startling in itself but because seeing it I for a moment did not dare look again towards Irma for fear that her beautiful hair had been singed off too, and perhaps her skin burned. I even called out stupidly, 'Are you burned?' before I looked at her and when I looked, I saw the reason I had hardly recognized her in the first place was that she had her jacket draped over her head with the sleeves knotted tight under her chin. I ran to meet them, the little girl howling, the little boy silent, seemingly in shock, Irma and Mr Buzbee each holding one of them by the hand.

'Are you burned?'

'Just on the hand,' she said. 'We have to get these children to the hotel with all speed and call an ambulance from there. They need to lie down right away and then be got to the hospital.'

'Could you,' said Mr Buzbee, the right side of whose face was lightly scarred by fire, 'carry the little boy? Something fell on my right wrist and I can't use it.'

I picked up the little boy whose clothes were tattered and charred in patches by the flames.

'I can't lift the girl,' said Irma, 'her body's burned somewhere and it hurts her to be carried.'

Not saying anything more we made our way as fast as we could towards the hotel. Although our route took us in the opposite direction from that in which the Town Hall lay, it passed beside a scruffy, treeless expanse of public park which ascended on that side all the way to the Town Hall. From a long way off I seemed to hear a faint hallooing, and looking over my shoulder saw at what must have been the window of the small Council chamber the head and shoulders of Harrogate leaning forward out of the window, his arm waving in a frantic and meaningless gesture. Gaining the shelter of the hotel, we laid the children as softly as possible on two of the broken-springed sofas in what was called the residents' lounge.

Irma said, 'The hell of it is I know nothing whatsoever about the treatment of burns. Anything we try to do for them may be the wrong thing. I'll ring for the ambulance and then try to get some instructions from the hospital.' She ran to the telephone.

Mr Buzbee knelt beside the little girl, who was now not howling but moaning, and stroked what was left of her hair gently with his left hand. The stench of charred clothes was horrible.

Returning from the telephone, Irma said, 'Mr Buzbee performed an act of unparalleled heroism.'

Buzbee, obviously in pain, managed a ghost of a smile. 'In the haste of the moment,' he said, 'and you, if you remember, actually pushed past me, went ahead.'

'Oh I was so glad,' Irma said to me, 'that you weren't there. You'd have pushed ahead faster still, recking not of the danger. You might have been burned to death. Naturally,' she added, 'I was anxious about Mr Buzbee, too.'

'I've heard,' said Mr Buzbee, 'that laying on big slabs of butter is a good thing for superficial burns.'

'Yes, yes,' said Irma. 'Now you say it I remember hearing that even long ago in Norway. I wouldn't dare risk it on the children in case it's the wrong thing, but we could try it on your face and my hand.'

I was already hurrying across the lounge, making for the kitchen, and after a few minutes' search for butter returned with a couple of pounds of it. Irma was scraping gently with her hands at thick patches of oily mess on the little girl's blouse

and skirt. 'It looks so disgusting, so filthy,' she said, 'it somehow shocks me to look at it.'

I handed Buzbee a slab of butter which he started to pat on
to the side of his face with his left hand. I lifted Irma's hand
by the wrist and spread butter thickly on the glaring red patch
which stretched from wrist to knuckles.

There was a thud of quick striding feet in the corridor and
Harrogate puffing a little, the ends of his moustache now actually pointing downwards as though in dismay, came through
the door.

'Well, well, well,' he said. "All the victims! My God what
a business! Allow me to congratulate you on what looks like
having been a pretty narrow escape. Nobody seriously hurt, I
hope?'

'I think the children may be seriously injured,' said Irma.
'And I think that Mr Buzbee's wrist is broken. We are both
burned a little, too, as you can see.'

'What a business,' said Harrogate again, stepping nervously
to and fro in the centre of the room. After applying the butter
to his face, Buzbee had been gently probing his right wrist
with the fingers of his left hand. 'Not broken, just sprained,
or perhaps a bruised bone,' he said.

'Devil of a thing to happen at a time like this,' said Harrogate. 'Fortunately, the television interviewer just telephoned
to say he'd be delayed a quarter of an hour or so at his hotel
waiting for a call from London, so I had time to dash over
here. Naturally, I was horribly worried when that waiter of
yours told his story about the fire.' With his hands behind his
back he walked from one couch to the other, standing beside
each in turn looking down in frowning thought at the charred
and oily clothes of the two children.

'There's just one point,' he said, 'which I'm sure you'll
absolutely appreciate. I want to be perfectly frank about this.
It wouldn't look at all good, I mean it wouldn't be conducive
to anything, very, very definitely the opposite in fact, if that
television fellow just happened to be passing by here on his
way to the Town Hall, when these children were being taken

out to the ambulance. I mean that sort of fellow, come right down to it, is no more nor less than a journalist, and you know what journalists are. If you don't, take it from me. Fellow like that sees an ambulance, sees a couple of stretchers being brought out of the hotel with two children on them and next thing you know he's looking them over, looking for copy, you know, that's what they call it, they'll do anything for that, and asking questions and then the fat's in the fire, if you follow what I have reference to.' He looked keenly at me and added, ' I mean to say, *verb sap*. Get me?'

'You mean the oil?' I said.

'Exactly,' said Harrogate. 'Bright lad.'

'I don't understand what you're talking about,' Irma said.

'Your bright-eyed spouse does,' said Harrogate heartily.

I said, 'Part of Mr Harrogate's interview deals with the matter of how the people and public services of this town under the direction of the Town Council successfully repelled the oil menace from that tanker and kept our beaches clean.'

'Exactly,' said Harrogate again. 'What I mean to say, we don't want to spoil the ship for a ha'porth of tar, do we? No pun intended. So what I had in mind to come over here to very, very tentatively suggest was just that if that ambulance you say you've sent for should happen to turn up within the next quarter of an hour or so, it might be advisable, taking everything into consideration, to get the ambulance men in here and ask them, use my name if you like, to delay the actual removal of the children for just a little while. As a matter of fact I don't think they look too bad and a few minutes' delay won't do them any harm.' He leaned forward suddenly over the couch where the little girl was lying, and said, 'Well, how are you feeling now, sweetheart? Not so bad, eh? More frightened than anything, I expect? Upsy-daisy. Chins up.' To my astonishment and I must say disgust, Irma positively beamed at him. She got up from the couch where she had been sitting beside the child, smiling and actually patting him on the back.

77

'I think,' she said, 'that's a very constructive suggestion indeed. We absolutely must not, how do you say? Spoil the ship for a ha'porth of tar. We must not allow the callous intervention of a journalistic hack to undermine your enterprise.'

'Well, thank you very much indeed,' said Harrogate, beaming too. 'I felt sure you'd see the thing my way. It's a pleasure when you get people who can weigh up one consideration against the other, get their priorities right. And whatever way you look at it,' he added, 'you can't help realizing that these two children are entirely responsible for this unfortunate thing that's happened to them. I mean to say, playing Buddhist priests! It very definitely amounts to delinquency. Well, I must be getting along. And what about you? You're all invited to watch the show, just a few friends to make up what they call the studio audience.'

'I'm afraid I'll have to stay with the children,' Irma said. 'And Mr Buzbee ought to go to hospital too and have that wrist looked at.'

'Well, I suppose it can't be helped,' said Harrogate grudgingly. 'But,' he said turning to me, 'you'll come back to the Town Hall, won't you? There's nothing you can do here, so far as I can see.'

A moment before I should have declined his invitation with some heat. But as he had turned to the door, displaying the back of his fawn jacket, I saw that it was not only heavily spattered with oily grease, but that in two places there adhered to it sizable lumps of black and stinking stuff. It was plain that Irma while she seemed to be congratulating him so heartily, had not only smeared her greasy hands on his shoulder blades but had contrived to scoop these lumps off the child's skirt and transfer them to Harrogate's back. She now looked at me gravely and said, 'I think it would be only proper for you to be present on this occasion which may be regarded as historic in the annals of our town. It will, I hope, be memorable and as Mr Harrogate says, there is really nothing that you can usefully do here.'

'There you are,' said Harrogate, 'your good lady's right

again. Come on, we have to hurry.' He turned at the door to wave his hand. 'Good-bye for now,' he sang out. 'Happy landings!'

The whiff of Harrogate's back reached my nose faintly even on the open street and in the narrow back stairway by which we entered the Town Hall, it became more noticeable still. 'Don't want to push through that crowd,' said Harrogate. 'This brings us out right on to the dais. I'll go right to my chair and you can nip across and join the others beyond the cameras.'

The interviewer, as it turned out, was already present and showing impatience. The director, the cameraman, the man in charge of the lighting and the man in charge of sound were all twitching, too, in their varying ways. They conveyed an air of hostility, as though someone had behaved rudely to their machines. There was a short delay while the camera was properly positioned in relation to Harrogate, who sat in a mayoral-type chair, resting his hand in a statesman-like manner on the smaller chair which he had placed carefully beside him with its back to the audience and camera. The interviewer sat a little in front of him and to the side. While the technicians completed their preparations, I found myself being addressed by Farragut, whom I found occupying the chair next to mine. 'Everything OK?' he said hoarsely, 'I hope that fire brigade that I had the presence of mind to call for got there in time. Nobody could say I didn't do my best.'

I said I supposed the brigade had got there long ago. At any rate there seemed to be none of the commotion outside the now curtained windows of the Council chamber which would certainly have occurred if the fire had taken hold. 'Well, all's well that ends well,' said Farragut. 'What I was afraid of there might have been a holocaust with the four burned to a cinder. I did think Mr Harrogate was taking a bit of a chance when he telephoned the brigade to take the longer way round. Just a matter of a few minutes though. No harm done.'

'He did what?' I said.

'He didn't want them roaring down the street, attracting undesirable attention, he said, just when this telly man was on the way. He told them to go round the back doubles.'

After the routine introduction of Harrogate, the interviewer started in with some genially encouraging questions. Harrogate, who by this time had got his moustache back into its horizontal or executive position, looked at him with an expression which conveyed that here was a man who had battled strongly, calmly and courageously with the furies of hell and emerged triumphant from the fray. In a West Country accent slightly more marked than he customarily employed, words oozed out of him in a verbal drip drip that had a slightly hypnotic effect upon me so that I hardly distinguished one bit of balderdash from another. Somewhere along the line I heard him say in reply to some question by the interviewer: 'Well yes, I won't deny that there were a couple of hours there when things looked very, very tricky. It was a time to muster all the resources, material and, if I may say so, spiritual, at our command. To put it in one word, what the situation called for was guts. That's a plain spoken English word which I think some people nowadays are just a little inclined to forget. What did we do? I'll tell what we did.'

At this point he rose slowly from his chair, while the cameraman, evidently forewarned, followed the movement with his instrument. 'We,' boomed Harrogate, spacing out his words, 'took ... off ... our ... coats.'

So saying, he got out of his jacket in what must have been a much-practised movement and swiftly draped it over the back of the smaller chair, placed there, as was now evident, for that purpose. 'We,' he continued, 'rolled ... up ... our ... sleeves.' The interviewer and the cameraman must have seen the back of that jacket simultaneously. To judge by the abrupt sniff he gave, the interviewer could actually smell it. A moment later the people in the front rows of the audience were goggling at the jacket, too. Extending his now bare forearm, Harrogate said, 'And what I want to tell each and every one of you that's interested enough to be watching me here tonight, is that it seems to me that what this country needs to do in this testing time we're going through is to take off our coats and roll up our sleeves and get on with the job of putting the situation right.'

Ten

I think the cameraman had actually taken a shot of the coat
itself. A moment later a small hubbub and confusion broke out
in the front rows of the audience as people shifted their admir-
ing gaze from Harrogate to the astonishing spectacle of this
coat with its ugly decoration of oil, the smears and blobs
arranged on it like booby-medals for services not rendered,
and their chairs shifted and squeaked under them as they craned
and peered.

I daresay all might have been well for Harrogate had he not
become aware, despite the glare of the lights which blurred
his view of the audience, that he had somehow lost their attention. His overweening vanity was bruised. He paused in mid-
sentence to glare as though at an outbreak of heckling. Then,
sensing that the coat was somehow the cause of this disturbance
and distraction, he bent forward to peer at it, thus offering the
camera what was almost a close-up of nothing but the top of
his head. The director snapped out a furious order to cut. The
camera stopped turning. Harrogate, author thus of his own
downfall, straightened himself and stood looking this way and
that in furious bewilderment. With equal fury the director and
interviewer closed in on him. In the confusion and excitement,
I and a couple of other citizens from the front row hurried
forward and invaded the dais.

'What's all this?' Harrogate was saying.

'You may well ask,' snarled the interviewer, ripping off the smoothly velvet glove his voice had worn for his public questioning. 'Are you trying to make fools of the public?'

Glaring down at the coat from close quarters, he and the director both twitched their noses in loud and offensive sniffs.

'Do you think you're being funny?' the director demanded. 'Is this your miserable idea of a joke? You've spent several minutes of valuable television time telling the world how, owing to your splendid and far-seeing arrangment of booms and barriers at the harbour mouth, you prevented oil ever getting near your beaches. Then you display a brand new jacket, which you certainly wouldn't have been wearing even if you ever were out in a boat directing the operations, covered with oil and, now I come to look at it closely,' he squatted down to examine the jacket more closely, 'there's sand mixed up with the oil. That came right off your beach, didn't it, Mr Harrogate?'

The points of Harrogate's moustache were already leaving the horizontal and turning downwards like flags lowered in mourning or surrender.

'I tell you I don't know anything about it,' he said.

'Is that so?' said the director, nastily.

'But look here,' said Harrogate in desperation, 'couldn't I put a bit in my speech saying that coat got that way when I was out fighting the menace?'

'Bollocks to that,' said the interviewer. 'Do you think the public's as big a fool as you seem to be?'

'Look here,' Harrogate began.

The interviewer interrupted him.

'Are you supposed to have gone around wearing that coat ever since the tanker business? Or were you keeping it as a sacred relic? If that's the impression you want to give the public, you'll look more of a monkey than you do already.' Harrogate was too agitated to object to this further insult. Instead he pleaded.

'But they cut films,' he said. 'They cut them in the cutting room. Everyone knows that. Why can't we cut this bit out and carry on? Sort of sew the two bits of the film together?'

'Thank you very much for your valuable suggestion,' said the director. 'We've already spent quite enough time and money on this low farce. It seems quite clear to me that you have deliberately attempted, for reasons which I can imagine, to deceive not only the general public but our organization. It's been misled into sending a team down here. We certainly don't propose to aid and abet your conjuring tricks any further. This is a total write-off. Good-day to you.'

'I congratulate you,' said the interviewer, 'on producing about the smallest non-event in the history of television. Good-day.' Nodding to the cameraman, who immediately began to dismantle his apparatus, the pair stepped together off the dais and strode away down the chamber.

Harrogate stood looking after them as one stupefied. Farragut saw fit to say, 'Hard cheese, Mr Harrogate. Still, these things happen. That's life on this earth. No use swimming against the tide, you know. Spit in the wind and you get an eyeful.'

The dull thud of these flat-footed statements served to rouse Harrogate from stupefaction to rage.

'Shut up!' he shouted, trying at the same time to pull up his moustache ends, which, however, failed to respond.

'What d'you mean, these things happen? They *don't* happen.'

'They have just happened, haven't they?' Farragut pointed out, angered in his turn.

Harrogate shouted that they bloody well shouldn't have. He shouted that something had been going on around there. He'd been made a victim of victimization. Somebody had got at that coat and what he asked was *cui bono*? In other words, who had an interest in wrecking this television show which would have done so much to put this town squarely on the map of the public consciousness? He shouted that there were certain people along the coast that were jealous of this town and of its success and that he wouldn't put it past them at that.

'Could be,' said Farragut. 'One thing you can say for sure is people have bad characters. You couldn't trust your twin brother if there was any money in it.'

While giving ear to these exchanges, I had taken the opportunity to examine the coat at close quarters, and was happy to note that Irma had at least not left anything in the way of a signature on it; no pattern of a small broad hand was visible. Nor did Harrogate, who at the time had been totally absorbed in his plan to keep the children under wraps, so to speak, and out of sight of the television interviewer, seem to have any recollection of her fulsome pats on the back, amounting to the equivalent of Judas-kisses. But though his reason seemed to be reeling under the shock of his recent surprises and disappointments, he was still evidently capable of a little elementary detective work. He startled me by suddenly turning in my direction and saying, 'Look lad, could one of those bloody children who caused all the trouble have been putting on an act? Lying there like half-dead, and then when my back was turned could have crept up somehow and smeared my coat?'

'It seems extraordinarily unlikely,' I said, guardedly.

'Could be,' said Farragut. 'Kids are born dishonest.'

An idea seemed to strike Harrogate with such effect that his moustache ends twitched and raised themselves a half-inch or so as though injected with some energy-giving fluid. He extended his forefinger sharply as though about to put it on some essential point. 'What about,' he said, 'what about that fellow that was around in your lounge? Stranger to me. I saw him somewhere about the town a week or two ago. Not the type of face I'd take on trust. He might,' he babbled excitedly, 'have been an agent for some of those fellows along the coast.'

I put on a dubious look.

'You think that's far-fetched?' Harrogate demanded vehemently. 'You're inclined to dismiss it as a mere figment? Let me tell you something. In this age of fierce, I might say internecine competition, you get spies and agents everywhere.

Look at this agency over there in the USA that infiltrates everything. Take industry. Industrial spies. It goes on all the time. Who is this fellow anyway?'

'He's a gentleman from Ireland who booked in yesterday at my hotel,' I said. 'But I don't think . . .'

Harrogate gave out with an hysterical snarl. 'Irish!' he said, 'well, there's a pointer right at the start. You know what the Irish are. Talk about the Pakistanis, the Irish are just as bad. Worse, I dare say. Been at it longer. Leaving their own country and battening on the openhearted generosity of poor old England. Natural-born sneaks and traitors. Sell themselves to anyone for what they'll fetch. No principles, no loyalty, no sense of gratitude. You know,' he shouted, his mind seeming to come adrift from its moorings and run wildly before the wind of his emotion, 'what they did to us in the war? Do you know how many of our fine West Country sailor lads were torpedoed and drowned in the waves of the Atlantic because Mr Irish de Valera wouldn't give us the use of those ports over there that we built long ago with our own sweat and blood? Can you tell me how many of them perished within sight of safety, while the Irish stood on the cliffs laughing at them and not lifting a finger to save them?'

'I'm afraid I've no idea.'

'Anyway, it was a hell of a lot,' said Harrogate. 'And this fellow that's sneaked into town is Irish, you tell me.'

It really seemed that Harrogate in his crazed temper might be going to call for some kind of a lynching party, or at least embark on a course of action which could be vexatious to Mr Buzbee. I said as calmly as possible, 'Irish or not, I really don't see how he could have had anything to do with this. I was in a position,' I said truthfully, 'to see everything that everyone did in our lounge all the time you were there. I am prepared to swear that Mr Buzbee was never within several feet of you.'

'Well, if you say so,' said Harrogate reluctantly. He added, with total irrelevance, 'He may have had nothing to do with this, but he'll bear watching all the same.' He babbled on for a little until he remembered that what he had to do now was to flatter and threaten the reporter for their local newspaper, explaining how unhelpful it would be for the town, and that reporter's future, if mention were made of any of the recent events.

On returning to the hotel, I found that the ambulance had borne away the two children and Mr Buzbee. Mrs Buzbee had followed it to the hospital in their car. Irma was alone, curled gracefully on a sofa in the room we used as our private sitting-room, smoking a small cigar and in the process of memorizing, as was her daily practice, two pages of the Concise Oxford Dictionary of Current English. As I entered she put her finger on the place she had reached and said, 'Faucal, F-A-U-C-A-L. Of the throat, deeply guttural. From the Latin F-A-U-S-E-S, throat, plus A-L.' I embraced her fervently, expressing my general love and my particular admiration for her achievement of the morning. She listened with keen pleasure to my detailed account of the 'non-events'.

'And he doesn't so much as suspect me, the avenging angel who laid him low and rolled him in the dust? He suspects nothing?'

'He suspects everything and nothing,' I said. 'Not you, at any rate for the moment, but the affair will ferment in the cess-pool of his subconscious mind. At the best he will subconsciously associate us with his humiliation.'

'It matters?'

'Perhaps. In a sense, I mean, that he will feel, even if vaguely, an increased hostility to myself and anything I may propose to him. The hostility, naturally, exists already; it is provoked by the necessity of constantly thinking of reasons to set my civic proposals aside. He feels guilt, too, because my proposals are good and his reasons for trying to shelve them are bad. He may even try, again obeying the promptings of his smutty subconscious, to make some definitive counter-move. He might, for example, try to get some resolution passed by the Council which would somehow, I have not thought out the details of his possible move, tie the hands of such members of the Council as might be inclined to support my scheme.'

'This being the posture of affairs,' said Irma, 'it behoves you to do what?'

'To press forward with increased speed and vigour on all fronts.'

Through a cloud of cigar smoke, she made wide round eyes at me.

I heard the telephone ringing in my office across the corridor. I hurried from the private lounge to my office, heard the exchange inform me that there was a call for me from London, and almost immediately was listening to Mrs Fitzpayne herself explaining that for 'very, very important reasons,' she had had to leave for the capital immediately after the conversation with Mr Ashleigh Groom, the previous afternoon, and was likely to be detained there for at least a week. My ejaculations of surprise and disappointment were entirely sincere. I had no need falsely to assume such emotions for her benefit. I have not, I think, concealed the fact that I had been physically dashed and put out by the frustration of the previous afternoon. I freely admitted to myself that what I may call 'the fringe benefits' accruing in terms of physical pleasure from the steady pursuit of my major objective, were in themselves highly attractive. Now they were to be postponed; postponed, so far as I could gather on the telephone, for an indefinite though possibly short period. The length of the period was to be decided, it seemed, by the course of the latest outbreak of guerrilla warfare between anti-tax activist Groom and the Inland Revenue. I made the distant telephone receiver in London throb with my passionate expostulations.

'But Ashleigh says,' said Mrs Fitzpayne.

'Damn Ashleigh!' I shouted. 'Will he never cease from troubling us? Are we to have no peace?'

'I know, I know,' she said. 'But you have to see it's all very, very important.'

After she had rung off, I had to sit quietly in the office for a few moments, sipping a glass of whisky, before I was capable of calmly estimating the pros and cons of this unforeseen development. After doing so and since the rains of May were falling vertically on the lawn this windless day, I invited Buzbee to join me in the office.

Eleven

He had returned from the hospital with his arm in a sling. 'Rather badly sprained but not broken,' he said, 'the children, they say, are as well as may be expected. Though just how well one may be expected to be after setting light to one's clothes and being more or less severely burned it's really hard to tell.'

'A reassuring phrase,' I said. ' Come to think of it, one might in that sense say that everyone in the world, whether half-starved, under bomb attack from the air, or just half-sick with worry about how they are going to stagger through the next year without going mad or bankrupt, is doing as well as can be expected.' 'Phrases of that kind,' Buzbee said, 'are used to perform psychological conjuring tricks; at least they are commonly used for that purpose in England. It would be interesting to know whether the Chinese do the same thing. Reports from somewhere or other repeatedly say that the people there are viewing the situation without "undue dismay". But given that a landslide is bringing half a mountain down on top of their village, or gangsters are roaming the streets of their town shooting and looting, just how much dismay ought to be considered "due"?

'I wonder,' continued Mr Buzbee, 'whether many children nowadays play Buddhist priests? Perhaps it has become a popular street game like hop-scotch or Guy Fawkes.'

'If so,' I said, 'it proves that the priests who originally incinerated themselves achieved at least something by way of an impact. In fact that would be true even if it's not a common game, even if only these two children here in our town were so vividly impressed.'

'But the question,' said Buzbee, 'is whether such an impression is worth making. Assuming, I mean, that it's to say the least of it very unlikely that the children had the least understanding of what the priests were burning themselves about.'

'In my opinion,' I said vehemently, 'it is always worth while to make an impact of some kind even if it is not understood. Like that, there is always the possibility of some kind of chain reaction being set off. If you wait to let out a yell until you are sure that everyone will understand what you are yelling about you may as well keep your mouth shut. In any case I suppose it is better that they should play at being Buddhist priests than being bombers in aeroplanes.'

Buzbee drank some whisky and seemed to reflect. He said, 'In my judgement those children were probably suffering from boredom. Their imaginations were groping around for something thoroughly un-boring to do. It may be that to pretend to be an avenger from outer space, or a cop or a robber has become boring. But one might say without much risk of exaggeration that to cover oneself with oil, drip petrol over it and then put a match to oneself must be at least a very un-boring thing to do. By the way, why weren't they in school?'

'Parents frequently send word to the school that their children are sick and, as in this particular case, send the children out to scavenge on the beach.'

'Is there much to be found on the beach?'

'You'd be surprised, I dare say, at the things people leave behind there. Umbrellas. Even, on a good day for the children, a camera. Brassières are commonly found. Once, it is not easy to construct the precise circumstances, a quite new pair of trousers. All such objects can of course be profitably sold. The parents no doubt pay the children some small commission, but you know that at least with children the routine even of money making is no absolute guarantee against boredom. I suppose these children made castles in the sand instead. That's how they got covered in the first place with the oil which Harrogate so cleverly and courageously prevented from reaching the beach at all. It was the sight of one another coated with oil which started the train of thought leading to the Buddhist priests.'

I had been speaking with my eyes half-closed by way of assisting the concentration of my thoughts. Opening them, preparatory to refilling our glasses, I noticed that the almost motionless clouds were now sitting down so thick and low that the room was in a depressing twilight, conducive to melancholy rather than keen or useful discussion of a given situation. I pressed the switch of the light on my desk. No light came.

I rang a bell. After some delay Farragut appeared.

All the lights on the ground floor, he told me, had fused. 'For no good reason that I can see,' he added. 'Nobody can say I am to blame. What I don't know about electricity and all that isn't worth knowing. Studied it man and boy since I was so high. You just stay where you are and I'll go and fix it.'

Buzbee looked after him thoughtfully. 'As Edwina says, a child of misfortune. I have noticed that he imagines everyone is going to blame him for everything.'

'He very often is to blame,' I said. 'That, of course, from his point of view is all the more unfortunate.'

'I gather from your wife,' Buzbee said, 'that he even managed to get blamed by Harrogate for reporting on the episode at the garage.'

'Maybe he did at that,' I said, 'that's the way Harrogate's mind works if work is the right word in connection with that particular bit of apparatus. He has probably got it in for you too.'

Buzbee gave a quick jerk to his glass, rattling the ice. 'How so?'

I explained how Harrogate had first suspected him of

'getting at' his jacket, how the information given by me to the effect that Buzbee was from Ireland had deepened these suspicions to the extent of producing a maniac outburst, and how I had finally testified as of my own knowledge that Buzbee had never been near the coat.

'Good,' said Buzbee.

I remarked that perhaps I had been wrong in making my statement about Ireland being Buzbee's place of origin. 'I recalled that you had disclosed to me that such was not in fact the case, but I assumed that since you had written "Ireland" in the visitors' book you would wish the same information to be given in response to the question "where is he from?"'

'I understand,' said Buzbee.

'Having been knocked half off his rocker by that interview coming apart in his hand and carrying around this notion that the Irish are a kind of premature Pakistanis or worse, and certainly a menace, he is liable to go on being suspicious of you in a general way. Of me too, as I have told Irma already. But so far as you are concerned what does it matter? What can he do?'

'One can't be too careful,' said Buzbee gravely. He let a brief silence intervene and then said, 'Don't *you* feel *you* can't be too careful?'

It seemed to me that as he said this he was rather ostentatiously not looking at me. I had the impression, too, that the tone of his question was meant to suggest to me that I should put a question in return; ask him what exactly he meant by that? While he sat, waiting perhaps for such a question from me, I experienced an unpleasant sensation.

I swallowed a little whisky quickly and said, 'I really don't think there is anything for you to worry about.'

This statement was of course untrue. If there was nothing for him to worry about, why was he worrying at all? And although his expression remained pensive rather than harried, he certainly was worrying somewhat about something.

The four of us: I and Irma, he and Edwina again lunched

together at the same table. Irma had already passed on to Edwina the news of events at the Town Hall. The topic seemed exhausted, or else Buzbee was for some reason anxious to exclude it from the conversation, preferring instead to start an immediate discussion of the use and purpose of fat or adipose tissue in the make-up of migratory birds.

'It is an astonishing although fairly well-known fact that quite small land-birds flying (as established by radar observations) at the rate of 25 mph, can fly non-stop for a distance of 1,000 and even of 1,500 miles. The energy and nourishment required for this barely credible undertaking is provided by a sudden increase in the volume of adipose tissue in the make-up of each bird occurring during the last ten days or week before the migratory flight begins. During this brief period each bird multiplies the amount of its fat by ten. And this,' Buzbee pointed out, 'is achieved not only by an intensive course of heavy feeding. A large proportion of it results from a change in the ratio of fat produced to food consumed. More of the food is transformed into fat than at other periods of the bird's life.

'You see,' he continued, 'what this might at least imply. The migratory flight, the purpose towards which the change in the bird's internal economy is directed, is still in the future. A present happening is caused by future events. Ought we to consider this phenomenon as an indication that, as is maintained by some modern philosophers, the cause of present events is determined not, as usually supposed, by the past but by the future? It is reasonable to assume that the bird is not conscious that tomorrow week it will have to fly 1,000 or 1,500 miles non-stop. At least it is unlikely that it is consciously preparing for it in the way a person is conscious when he packs his bag for a long journey. Yet the necessary internal changes seem to occur as effectively and inevitably as digestion. If such a thing can happen in the body of a relatively unconscious bird how much more might the full consciousness of a future objective affect the present mental and physical behaviour of a human being?'

We considered this matter at length, approaching it from various angles, advancing arguments for and against acceptance of Buzbee's tentative theory. As a result, when I retired to the couch in my study to take the siesta which I like to do when not interrupted, I found my brain over-excited and was forced to drink a quantity of brandy before I could sleep.

I was awakened a couple of hours later by the ringing of the telephone in the corridor. Buzbee must have been seated in the armchair provided for those using the telephone, for the ringing seemed hardly to have begun before his voice was heard, speaking very loudly, and saying, 'Yes, this is B speaking.'

I was sufficiently interested in Buzbee to have listened in any case; in fact if necessary I would have used the extension telephone on my desk for the purpose. However, being comfortably stretched on the couch I did not bother to do so since his voice was clearly audible through the door. I could not even be accused of eavesdropping. He said again:

'Yes, B speaking, are you ready?' This was asked in the manner of someone getting ready to make a report, and he paused as though giving someone at the other end time to get a pen and notebook ready. 'All right?' he said. 'Now listen – preliminary enquiries tend to confirm the Department's long distance estimate of the situation. By the way, I don't need to remind you, I suppose, to rush this to S S T D and of course keep a copy for my own file. OK? I now regard H as the primary, though not necessarily the final subject for enquiry by the Department. My preliminary investigations here have shown that there is *prima facie* reason to suppose that his activities and general methods have been along the lines surmised by the Department. I had occasion this morning to make brief personal contact with the individual in question. The circumstances of our meeting were somewhat unusual. It may be significant that H, as I have later learned, displayed in the presence of third and fourth parties, a notably hostile interest in my presence here. However, for reasons which I will specify in my written report, I am not of the opinion that H has any

95

knowledge of my actual purpose. Got that? That's all for now. Keep in touch.'

I heard him put down the receiver and his steps moving along the corridor towards the stairway. It seemed obvious, for a start, that he could not have been aware that anyone was overhearing him. He had, I realized, been speaking in a quite normal voice. Having noted that the corridor was empty except for his own presence, he might easily have been deceived by the mock-Tudor panelling of the corridor into supposing that its walls, though actually gimcrack, were solidly soundproof. I had known other guests commit sometimes embarrassing indiscretions over the telephone as a result of this misapprehension.

On the other hand it did strike me that a man giving what one had to assume was a confidential report of some kind to the organization he referred to as the Department which one must suppose was the Department also referred to by him as the S S T D, would have paid rather more attention to what is called security. Serious matters, I felt, should be treated more seriously. Rather unreasonably, perhaps, I could not help feeling some resentment on behalf of this unknown Department at the casual manner in which Buzbee seemed to be handling the affair, whatever it might be.

Setting aside these considerations for a moment, I brooded on the significance of the message itself. It was glaringly obvious from the context that the 'H' must be Harrogate. What then were the activities which Buzbee had been investigating? These, according to his telephone message, had been conducted before he had 'made contact' with Harrogate personally. But this contact had been made at eleven o'clock that morning. And Buzbee had registered at the hotel less than twenty-four hours earlier. Then I realized that this might well be a false premise. I vividly recalled, now, that Mrs Fitzpayne had on the previous day claimed to have seen Buzbee at least three times in the town within the previous week. At the time I had dismissed this assertion as the product of an imagination always over-heated by the sight, or even the thought of, what she called 'Government types'. It now occurred to me that I might well have been mistaken. Harrogate, too, I now remembered, in the course of his outburst that day at the Town Hall, had declared that he too had seen Buzbee lurking about the town.

Twelve

I saw that it was essential, however delicate or frustrating the task might be, to elicit some information from Buzbee himself.

In preparation for this attempt, I decided to concentrate for the next hour on seeking to recollect all that I could of his conversation during the brief period of our acquaintance. I should thus approach him, I felt, better equipped to assess his responses to whatever questions I might, subtly or bluntly, present him with.

As things turned out I had no opportunity for private conversation with him until quite late the following morning. For when Irma and I came into the dining-room that evening I noticed that the Buzbees, although it was early, were there before us and had established themselves at a small table for two. Apart from friendly greetings called across the room, we had no speech with them except when they left the dining-room at the end of dinner and mentioned in passing that the evening was so fine after the rain that they were going for a walk along the beach. An hour or more later we heard them return and go straight to their room.

In the morning, as we lay in bed drinking coffee I mentioned to Irma that I must be out and about early because I needed to have a word with Pete before ten o'clock, which was the hour when he received his first patient of the day.

'As I told you yesterday,' I said, 'vigorous action is necessary on all fronts. I wish to mobilize Pete's influence with the Town Council in case of any sly sudden move by the man Harrogate. Pete can be invaluable.'

'You will be too late,' said Irma. 'Edwina Buzbee told me yesterday that he has arranged to pick her up here in his car at nine-thirty and take her on a trip to the hinterland. Fresh woods and pastures new. Scenes of rural beauty followed by a cold collation at some hospitable hostelry.'

'How can he do that?' I exclaimed indignantly. 'What about his suffering patients? Are they to peer at life through maladjusted spectacles while their oculist gallivants? And what about my urgent business with him?'

'I don't suppose he knew you had any urgent business with him.'

'It never occurred to me as necessary to warn him that I might have. One doesn't expect a rising professional man to jump into his car at nine-thirty of a week-day morning and take off for a tour of the interior. It's little short of irresponsible. Grossly so.'

Driven by anger and determination, I was beginning to heave myself out of bed when I heard the light step of what could only have been Mrs Buzbee (for they were the only guests in the hotel) going eagerly past our door along the corridor; nine-twenty-nine. Irma had been right. I was too late. I relapsed against the pillows, only a little relieved by the fact that this *contretemps* gave me time to follow my usual practice of drinking a third large cup of coffee; this time laced with a little rum. It was not enough to abate my annoyance with Pete and, now I came to think of it, with Edwina Buzbee too. I sought to review calmly the facts in the situation. Thinking aloud, I pointed out to Irma that she was in a sense responsible for the present untoward developments. I realized that Pete must have cancelled all today's appointments yesterday morning in order to take Edwina for an outing. One could only conclude that Pete had been, as they say, bowled over by Edwina

Buzbee like an adolescent knocked silly by first love.

'What do you suggest we do?' asked Irma.

'Well, what of Buzbee? What are likely to be his reactions to the sight of my brother-in-law blatantly exerting himself to seduce his youthful wife? Naturally you are going to say that we have no assurance that she really is his wife. She may, as I remarked to you soon after their arrival, be his mistress. She may, if you insist on taking all possibilities into account, be his daughter. Your objection is irrelevant. In fact if either one of these two possibilities were to prove true, the likeliness of unpleasantness arising would be sharply increased. There is no certainty that Buzbee is the kind of man who would possibly tolerate the seduction of his wife. It is even more improbable that he, or any man, having taken the trouble to acquire as his mistress a nymphet barely out of her teens, or to establish an unusual and, legally speaking, dangerous relationship with his daughter, would lightly accept the destruction of his achievement at the hands of a Norwegian oculist with a sister-complex. I may say that I have begun to esteem Buzbee. I have even, with some reason, thought of him as a potential ally against the forces confronting me. Now, as a result of Pete's thoughtless, unbridled sexual lusts, the chances are that at the best Buzbee will up stakes, leaving us with the whole of our accommodation at the hotel unoccupied, instead of ninety per cent of it, and at the worst, that he will tend to regard us, along with Pete, as vexatious elements and hatch some scheme of revenge.'

'Such as?'

'If I knew that I should be better prepared to throw up a line of defence. As it is, all I can say is that in my view there is a great deal more to Buzbee than meets the eye.'

'You're talking about that telephone call you overheard?'

'That and other pieces of what seem to be a jigsaw puzzle, which are however still too few to enable us even to guess at the pattern or picture.'

I recalled his entry in the visitors' book and subsequent explanation of it, the fact that both Mrs Fitzpayne and Harrogate had claimed to have seen him in the town several times during the previous week, and his notable uneasiness when I had casually suggested that Harrogate looked upon him with suspicion and hostility.

'The posture of events,' said Irma, 'evidently presents a challenge.'

Reviewing the various courses of action which might be taken by way of meeting the challenge, I concluded that any 'action' in the narrow sense of the word was likely to produce the illusion of progress rather than progress itself. I therefore decided first to resume my reading of the book left behind by a last summer's visitor, which I have already mentioned. It was in fact a translation of a work by a French anthropologist. I was not at all familiar with the subject matter (which concerned an appraisal of what the author described as the 'savage' mind), and still less with the philosophical methods and terms involved and employed. It was thus heavy going for me, but paradoxically the heavier the going the more soothing I found it. Also, as I slowly pushed and stumbled my way from page to page, often falling, so to speak, flat on my face, and sliding or rolling through a half a paragraph in a state of stunned coma, I was aware of mysterious flashes of illumination in the fog through which I moved, of suggestive vistas briefly opening.

I hoped that with my body comfortably at ease in the bed, and with my conscious mind thus actively preoccupied with the book, my subconscious might just as actively get to work on preparing a solution of the practical problems which confronted me.

Our bedroom overlooked the garden. Towards midday my attention was distracted from the book by the faint sound of what seemed to be raucous laughter in the middle distance. On crossing the room to peer out of the open window on to the now sunlit lawn, I was astonished to see just emerging on to it from the steps, the figures of Buzbee and Harrogate, the latter apparently thumping the former's shoulder in jovial fashion and responsible for the laugh I had heard. To me it was as though, having sat through the first act of a play, one saw the curtain rise on a second act apparently transposed from a different play altogether. I had no clue as to the motivations and probable behaviour of the characters.

With Harrogate still laughing and thumping his jocular point home on Buzbee's shoulder, they crossed to a table beside the pool and seated themselves. A moment later Farragut appeared on the stage carrying a tray with glasses, a syphon and a bottle of liquor. I could see Harrogate going through elaborate gestures of 'playing host', pouring drink into Buzbee's glass, cautiously squirting in soda, watching for Buzbee's signal to stop. They then resumed the conversation, or rather Harrogate went on talking, more seriously now it seemed, while Buzbee listened with his head a little on one side and an occasional nod.

Fascinated by the scene and afraid that the characters might move off the stage again before I could acquaint myself with the meaning of this performance, I bathed, shaved and dressed with the utmost speed, and headed out to the pool.

They greeted me cordially. Buzbee with his warm but slightly austere smile, Harrogate with an enthusiasm as false as the bright teeth which I had heard he had had specially made for the purposes of his television interview. After a quick pumping of my hand and arm he was loping off across the lawn to call for Farragut to bring another glass for me.

'A little unexpected, all this?' I could not help saying to Buzbee. He looked at me with the same smile, shrugged slightly and occupied himself with the business of getting a cigarette out and using his lighter. Rejoining us, Harrogate got off some twaddle about delightful place you have here, wish I could come and enjoy it more often, on the run all day I'm afraid and where does that get any of us you may well ask etc., etc.

'I am sorry,' Buzbee said evenly, 'to hear about your interview. An unfortunate business. Have you probed the mystery yet?'

Harrogate waved his hand, decorated with an absurd cameo ring, in a dismissive gesture as obviously fraudulent as his greeting to me had been.

'Given up thinking about it,' he said. 'Not worth it. Accidents will happen, you know, in the best regulated Town Halls. Mind you don't quote me on that, I wouldn't like the ratepayers to hear me say that.' He turned on a laugh. I had by now noticed that the ends of his moustache were pointing upwards, an indication that this was a social occasion, a convivial little meeting between men of the world. Returning to me he said, 'I hear Norman here's making quite a long stay with you. As a summer visitor he is an early bird. And very nice for all concerned too. Good for the hotel business, and what I always say is that what's good for the hotels is good for the town. When it comes to the tourist season, what I say is "the earlier it starts the longer it lasts" if you see what I mean?' Farragut having brought the fresh glass, Harrogate poured me a drink and with continuing conviviality raised his own and said, 'Well, Norman, old boy, here's hoping you catch some nice worms. Old Chinese saying.'

Although my short acquaintance with Buzbee was at least three times as long as Harrogate's, it had never occurred to me to call him Norman. In fact, now I came to think of it, he was precisely the type of man whose manner, however cordial, by no means suggests an early approach to Christian name terms. Harrogate, as I knew from experience, considered that to call a man by his first name in itself somehow constituted a claim upon his intimacy.

Harrogate turned to politics, proclaiming optimistic opinions. He took the view that 'provided the public in general, and the working man in particular is prepared to put up with a slice of the cake commensurate with the needs of the nation as a whole,' we should all gradually pull through 'to more normal times.'

'Mind you,' he added, looking sternly at the tip of his cigarette, 'in my humble opinion one of the things this country is suffering from is what I call an inflated bureaucracy. Do you know what the increase is in the number of civil servants sitting on their little backsides in their little offices in Whitehall and all over, compared to what it was five years ago?'

'I imagine it is considerable,' said Buzbee.

'You bet it is considerable,' said Harrogate; 'I could quote you the figures if I had them. Pullulating, that's what these Government departments are doing. Nothing short of pullulating. You get a new department, a new set of initials, every damn day. Often enough they just give the initials and expect the poor bloody public to work out what they stand for. Just to give you an instance, only a week or so ago I saw a reference somewhere to some outfit calling itself the S S T D. I don't know what that stands for. Bet you don't either,' he said to Buzbee. 'Ever heard of it?'

Thirteen

Buzbee patted a lock of silver hair into place and said, 'Afraid not. But that means nothing. This outfit, as you describe it, may be well known, important, quite familiar to students of political affairs. But then I am simply not one of those. My interest in politics, such as it is, is confined to trying to guess whether our politicians are going to drag us into war next month or not until the year after next.'

With his telephonic report vividly in mind I recalled his earlier remark to me about people who pretended to have no interest in politics – 'the Heathen Chinee in the game'. Buzbee now added a few further banal remarks evidently designed to emphasize that this was a game he did not understand.

Harrogate spoke heartily, but seeming to speak off the top of his head while his thoughts were chugging along another line. 'You're damn right. It's all balls and bang-me-arse. Many's the time and oft, let me tell you, I've said to myself I've said I'd give my right arm to get right out of this whole game of politics which has its fascinations, mind you, but in the last analysis what's it all about? Get away somewhere and read and think and really live. Probably a man like you'd laugh just at the idea that a man like me has ideas outside the sordid rut and arena of politics. Nor would it do me any good with the voters to let them get the idea I was some sort of a dreamer of dreams with my head in the clouds. And talking of that,' he said, doing emphatic business with wrist watch, ' I mustn't sit here indulging myself, much as I enjoy a little bit of conversation that isn't limited to the town pump. Duty calls. Burden and heat of the day sort of business.'

He got to his feet, patted Buzbee on the shoulder and waved a hand at me. 'Be seeing you. If you can't be good be careful. Anything I can do, any time, ring me. Just part of the service.' Smiling with all his teeth, and waving his hand raised above his shoulder, he marched towards the hotel.

'A friend in need,' I said. Buzbee shrugged again in his fashion.

I had exercised restraint, curbed my supposed impetuosity several times in the last forty-eight hours. I did not feel inclined to do so again. Was I supposed to sit there for a half-hour or so, twirling on the earth's axis while our cells and tissues decayed minute by minute and – for the sake of conventional reticence – not pose to the man Buzbee at least some of the questions which crowded in upon my mind? A thousand times No.

'You don't,' I said, 'appear at all surprised by Harrogate's change of front. I therefore assume you know the explanation. I should be interested to know that explanation too.'

'Naturally,' said Buzbee. 'That's of course. Given the remarks he made to you about me there are natural reasons for your interest. I take leave, if you'll forgive me, to ask myself whether there are less obvious reasons too.'

'If this is cackle,' I said, intentionally very sharp, 'let me ask you to cut it.'

Buzbee said, ' Quite. I take it you listened in to a short telephone conversation I conducted from your hotel late yesterday afternoon?'

'There was no question of listening in,' I said, showing irritation. 'I'm not responsible for the acoustics of the hotel, and it is no fault of mine if you choose to disregard them. Anyone within fifteen yards of you could have overheard.'

'I have reason to suppose that everyone within that range

did. When I spoke of your "listening in" I used the phrase in no pejorative sense. I have no complaint at all, how could I? I was thinking of Farragut. I thought it likely that you were in your office. But I knew for a fact that Farragut was behind the door of his bar the other side of the corridor.'

Buzbee refilled his glass and said, as the soda gushed, 'You know that in Africa there is a species of bird known as the Tickbird. The function of the Tickbird is to settle upon the hides of mammals ranging from antelope to rhinoceros and peck away at their hides, relieving them of ticks and other parasites. In return for these services rendered the Tickbirds are assured they will not be disturbed while feeding by a lash of the tail or other annoyance. I have been told they even settle between the jaws of one or other of the great beasts – I forget which – and act as toothpicks. Farragut is one of humanity's Tickbirds.'

'So far,' I said, 'so good. But not very far yet.'

'I will go further fast. Farragut lives a precarious existence. His faculties of self-preservation are strained to find means of appeasing threatened hostility. That, as you told me, was his position vis-à-vis Harrogate following the scene at the Town Hall.'

'And so?'

'I too, though by no means for motives comparable to that of the Tickbird, was a little discommoded by what you told me of Harrogate's attitude to myself. You did not conceal, perhaps you did not try to conceal, your surprise at the attention I paid to that information.'

'It puzzled me. I asked you, as I recall, what it could matter to you.'

'And I said that one could not be too careful. After reflection I decided that my best policy was to mount a counter-attack. If it is permissible to describe as a counter-attack one which takes place before any attack has got going. I decided to throw a scare into Harrogate. Make him jump.'

'In his case always an excellent idea.'

'It combined business with pleasure.'

'I am still in the dark.'

'Briefly . . .' said Buzbee.

His explanation was not brief, but it was comprehensive. He reminded me unnecessarily of the sufficiently common-place fact that the huge majority of humans live their lives in the more or less conscious, more or less vivid, fear of something or other. He mentioned cancer of breast or lung, atomic fall-out, public or private humiliation, the death of loved ones. These, at least in non-primitive societies, were classifiable as general fears not much affected by the divisions of class or economic status. There were also more particular fears, for the most part confined to particular economic groups. Members of the so-called working class feared unemployment, short time working, and loss of pay due to illness.

'In our society at least,' said Buzbee, 'the rest of the community is afflicted by one overriding terror, the terror of the tax man. Half their working lives, half their mental activities are devoted to eluding, circumventing, or appeasing the tax man.'

Thinking of Mrs Fitzpayne, I broke in to agree with him emphatically. I mentioned her as striking evidence of a situation which was in any case sufficiently obvious. He broke off his exposition, and seemed to meditate briefly on these remarks of mine. 'Is that so?' he asked. 'You are not exaggerating, over-dramatizing?'

'Certainly not,' I said. 'But let us not be diverted to a side issue.'

'No no, of course,' Buzbee said. 'Interesting, all the same. However, as I was saying . . .'

One could take it for granted that under the impulse of this particular terror eighty per cent of those liable to direct taxation had, at some time or another, committed some illegal act, or, which in this respect came to the same thing, an act which they believed to be a cunningly illegal act designed to outwit the tax man. 'They are all, therefore,' he said, 'either potential gaol birds or believe themselves to be so. They all have skeletons in their cupboards.

'If this is true of that whole eighty per cent, how much more certainly is it true of a greasy rogue like the man Harrogate? To frighten him, to make him jump, to reduce him to the nervous crawl just witnessed, it was only necessary to suggest that someone had a key which might fit his cupboard: was perhaps already trying to insert it in the lock. Just recall to mind the tenor of my conversation on the telephone. You will immediately see that it was calculated, if overheard by Harrogate, to produce that desirable result. Obviously there was no way of arranging for him to overhear it personally. In any case the necessary alarm and despondency would be sharply increased if he supposed that I imagined myself to be talking confidentially, without any idea that my conversation would be reported to him. A report reaching him in that way would strike him as menacingly authentic.

'Having established general principles of my strategy, it remained only to translate them into practice. Immediately after lunch yesterday I arranged with Edwina that in the course of the afternoon she should drive twenty miles or so along the coast and at a pre-concerted time telephone to me here at the hotel. By taking a drink in your bar and mentioning casually to Farragut that I was expecting a highly important telephone call I made virtually certain that he would remain in the bar. He would act on the general principle that eavesdropping on a confidential call can never do harm and may do good. He would at once see that the call related to Harrogate. By sneaking off in his general capacity as tickbird to Harrogate with the news he would be in a position to expect some reward for services rendered, even if the reward took the negative form of non-malevolence on the part of Harrogate towards himself. The result of this manoeuvre you have just seen. The speed and nature of Harrogate's reaction certainly indicated that the skeleton is a large one.'

I could not refrain from clapping my hands gently together in sheer pleasure.

'And these initials? SSTD?'

'In my view,' said Buzbee, 'they stand for Special Supervisory Tax Detachment. To begin with I thought of the final D as standing for Department. In fact as you may have noticed I referred to the Department in my conversation. But while actually doing so it occurred to me that Detachment was more forceful, has a more sinister ring. It evokes vague images of a secret police. You agree?'

I agreed heartily.

'What we have here,' continued Mr Buzbee, speaking as though he were commenting on a case reported in the newspapers, 'is an example of what might be classified as the confidence trick in reverse. One might almost call it the no-confidence trick. For the successful operation of the ordinary confidence trick two elements are, by the well-known, indeed classic, rules of the game, essential. The first is that the victim must have that quality described by a scholarly student of the operation as "larceny in the blood". The possibility of pulling, as they say, a fast one on society must represent to him an irresistible temptation.

'The mere suggestion that there is a way of secretly tunnelling under the barbed wire fence of restrictive social regulations, a way of bluffing the guards at the gate by an exercise of superior intelligence, excites simultaneously his stupidity and his vanity. Since all such tunnellings and such bluffs are, *ex hypothesi*, illegal or at least on the shady side of the law, it is usually the business of the professional confidence trickster to draw attention, lightly but unmistakably, to this aspect of the matter in hand. If it were represented as being entirely above board the victim's suspicions might be aroused. Nor would it appeal to that element of vanity which causes a quite extraordinary number of people to believe, without any justification, that they would if they so chose be more successful as criminals than the detected criminals they so frequently read about.

'The vulgar image of the confidence trickster and his victim,' continued Buzbee, 'is that of a cunning swindler deceiving a simple, honest man. Not so. The other essential element is the one ordinarily emphasized in reports of such swindles.

It is necessary for the trickster to gain the trust of the victim. And here again obviously the attraction for the victim of shady business plays an important role. I believe the records show it to be the case that in many instances the victim does not in point of fact unquestioningly and naïvely swallow the trickster's own story. The victim may even recognize that the man who is offering him a chance to make an easy fortune by outwitting society or some factor of society has some criminal qualities. But at a fairly advanced stage of the game the existence of these qualities becomes in itself an attraction, almost an additional ground for trust and co-operation. In other words the victim wants to latch on to the other's criminal qualities and draw advantage from them.

'In the no-confidence trick the situation is, as I have said, reversed. The operator, in this context I prefer that word, substitutes for the larceny in the blood the certainty that there is a skeleton in the victim's cupboard. And instead of gaining the victim's trustful co-operation, he works by exciting mistrust, suspicion and fear. In this situation too the victim's belief in the more or less criminal character of the operator works to the operator's advantage. He believes, that is to say, that if the operator has the key to the skeleton cupboard, he will not hesitate to use it. Thus he in a sense saves the operator the trouble and risk of blackmailing him, by constructing a situation in which the victim puts together out of his own fears a sort of blackmail-yourself kit. Without being positively blackmailed he is compelled to behave as though acting under that type of duress. On the part of the operator it is the practice of a kind of jujitsu in which the victim's own weight, or rather his character and his past, send him flying through the air to tumble flat on the mat.'

Fourteen

'So there you are.' Buzbee concluded his talk like a lecturer rolling up his chart and laying down his pointer.

Naturally I was much delighted and stimulated. First by the imaginative conception of his plan, secondly by the deft assurance by which it had been carried out, and thirdly by the sound, if slightly pedantic, exposition of the basic principles involved in the operation of the no-confidence trick. It seemed to me that there were certain affinities between this man's thinking and my own. He had the quality, it appeared to me, of clearing certain vistas which had hitherto been obscured or shadowed.

He had put me under an obligation, and I cast about in my mind for some means of repaying this debt.

It was difficult, like selecting a present for an acquaintance of whose tastes you know little except that they seem likely to be discriminating. For this reason I decided at once to eliminate from my thoughts any resentment I might have been inclined to feel at the fact that he had now the air of having explained the entire situation, including his own motivations, to the satisfaction of any reasonable man. But, absolutely without resentment, it had to be admitted that his explanation was not entirely full. On one point, at least, it was less than wholly candid.

Although he had referred to, had even underlined the fact of his own disquiet at my mention of Harrogate's originally hostile attitude to himself, he had swept this disquiet under the carpet, with no more said about it than that 'one can't be too careful' or words to that effect. I made up my mind that within a few minutes I would proceed to fulfil my obligations by parcelling up and making him a gift of my own knowledge of the state of affairs which just possibly might be of some practical use to him, though I could not imagine what that could be, and to include in the parcel, as a sign of confidence and good will, a frank avowal of my own motives and objectives. But since I had this gift already half-wrapped for a presentation I felt justified in putting to him a question.

I asked him point blank just why he had been so disquieted by my report of Harrogate's attitude. All very well, I said to come out with a phrase such as 'one cannot be too careful' but the use of such a phrase could have one of two implications: Either, I said, it implied that he was of a neurotically nervous cast of mind; the sort of man, I remarked, who in a mid-Eastern hotel might insist on seeing the drinking water boiled in front of him. Even on the strength of a slight acquaintance I took leave to doubt whether this was true of him. Or what he meant was that he personally had special reasons for being careful. Did he mean, I asked smiling, that he too had some small skeleton in his cupboard?

I awaited his reply anxiously, afraid that this remark might indicate not only a vulgar inquisitiveness, but a lack of appreciation of the confidence he had shown in me by his account of his recent behaviour. To my relief he smiled more warmly than usual.

'Naturally,' he said. 'Almost everyone either has a skeleton in his cupboard or believes that inside the cupboard there is something which other people would take to be a skeleton if they saw it, which comes to the same thing.' He stopped smiling and said, 'I should have thought *you* would have appreciated that.'

Buzbee continued, 'Having disposed of Harrogate, I would

like, if I may, just to refer back to a remark you made about Mrs Fitzpayne. You said, I think, that she too is a notable victim of what I have called the terror of the tax man. Could you expand that?'

It was, I saw, the cue for me to hand over my gift. I said, 'I would prefer to do so within the framework of a wider context.'

'I shall be delighted,' said Buzbee courteously, refilling our glasses and setting himself back in a posture of relaxed attention. I drank deeply and spoke.

I began by pointing out that Mrs Fitzpayne was only incidentally relevant to the campaign on which I was engaged. It was simply her possession of this mansion and spacious estate with many outbuildings on the outskirts of our town, and the circumstances under which she had come to possess it, which brought her as an individual into the campaign at all. In order therefore to understand her particular relevance it was necessary to view the matter in the fullest possible perspective. Bearing that in mind, it was possible to approach that same matter from either of two directions; from, so to speak, the immediately practical towards the ultimately possible, or from a survey of the ultimately possible to an examination of the immediately practical steps that could be taken towards its achievement.

'The first order would be best, I should say,' said Buzbee.

I was glad to hear him say so. It was the approach I would myself have chosen. Finding myself excited by the opportunity to express myself fully to a comparative stranger, I found it impossible to remain seated. I rose from my chair, placed one foot on the seat of it, and rested my forearm across my knee.

Buzbee contemplated the sea and then said, 'And your immediate plan?'

'By means,' I said, 'considered but not yet wholly frowned upon, I cause Mrs Fitzpayne to evacuate her house. By way of manoeuvres which I will not bother to detail at this juncture, the property is thrown more or less forcibly, more or less against the will of such specimens as Harrogate, into the possession, into the lap as the saying goes, of the Town Council. It becomes available, in the first instance, as a spacious accommodation for classrooms, laboratories, libraries and recreation grounds for the at present miserably served school-children (whatever type of school they may be attending), of the town. You will at once object that given the tangle of laws, bylaws, and other regulations affecting our educational system, given the inevitable conflict of political and financial interests both the local and national, we have no guarantee that the mere existence of this accommodation will result in its being practically used for the desirable purpose. Naturally, if you regard this Sargasso Sea of resistance as existing in a state of invulnerable inertia, you would be right. My point is first that just as an atomically powered vessel might be driven disruptively into the Sargasso Sea, so persistent individual action can penetrate this other mess, and shove it about into useful and meaningful shape. Secondly, a moment's reflection will certainly convince you that the mere existence of this accommodation, provided by the evacuated mansion of Mrs Fitzpayne, will itself provide precisely that leverage, that source if you like, of atomic energy to power the boat, with which it is indispensable and would prove irresistible. It is one thing for Harrogate and his kind to assert, using their favourite excuse for squalid inaction, that economic and other conditions leave us no alternative but to continue to put up, or rather to force the children to put up, with existing conditions, quite another if the material existence of that vacant house on its plateau, daily demonstrates to one and all that their excuse is patently invalid.

'The flabby council of the Israelites regularly voted to advise their community to live in bondage because there was nothing else to do. When Moses produced his proverbially well-illustrated brochure, complete with map, of the Promised Land, their position became indefensible. With the Promised Land in full mental view all but the most timid or those who were making a good thing as hangers on and agents of Pharaoh, the eternal Uncle Toms, decided to take a chance to have, as they say, a bash. Here too the conviction that a bash must be had will, if skilfully imparted and actively stimulated, become irresistible.'

Fifteen

'You comprehend immediately how, once these heights are gained, it will become apparent that they are only preliminary gains establishing strong positions from which to proceed to further advances.'

'Children,' said Mr Buzbee, 'are a good lever. Nobody cares openly to proclaim opposition to their welfare and interests.'

'Of course,' I said. 'In our society everyone publicly proclaims that the interests of the rising generation are paramount, while in fact pushing them somewhere near the back of the financial queue or at least behind moon-flights, space-flights, military missiles of all kinds and the researches necessary to perfect offensive and defensive methods of germ warfare. My plan, and I declare it true even though you may privately consider that I exaggerate its importance, will call the bluff – first locally, then in wider spheres.'

'No suggestion that you exaggerated,' said Mr Buzbee.

'It follows,' I said, 'not as night follows day, but as the collection of the winnings follows a well-considered bet, that although the welfare of children is the immediate gain to be obtained, it is – looked at in either way – simply a jumping-off ground, a long lever, as I have said, to lift a great mass.'

'Coming down to brass tacks,' said Mr Buzbee . . .

'I was about to suggest that we do so,' I said.

'Well then, as regards Mrs Fitzpayne. The relations which one may assume to exist, or to be about to exist between yourself and Mrs Fitzpayne are, I take it, to be viewed as part of your general plan?'

I said, 'Not perhaps an entirely indispensable part but, in my estimation, useful.'

'In other words, if I may put it in somewhat plain terms, your feeling is that when you lay Mrs Fitzpayne you are, as it were, laying for England? For civilization itself?'

'You exactly expressed my thoughts.'

'But since you do not regard this as the absolutely essential part of your hold, if I may so describe it, upon Mrs Fitzpayne, I take it you have some other means of leverage?'

I said, 'I have all along, now that I look at the matter clearly, been more or less unconsciously proceeding in accordance with the principles which you have only just now helped me to formulate more clearly. I refer to your remarks about the terror of the tax man. As I have already told you Mrs Fitzpayne is peculiarly susceptible to this particular terror. For the past several weeks I have been seeking to blow so hard upon the sparks of this terror as to puff it into a blaze. It has been my purpose to suggest to her that although she believes herself to have, so to speak, advanced far and fast into the tax collectors' territory and her victorious occupation of Moscow to be the result of her successful strategy, her position there is hideously precarious. And naturally I have at the same time tried to convey to her that, if she will listen to my advice in time, if she will sell out for a song and, cutting some immediate losses, reputed to save her position, she may yet do so without the loss of more than a few stragglers from the Grande Armée of her financial resources.'

Buzbee said, 'You are, I should say, on a safe wicket. What you tell me confirms my own, admittedly, speculative estimate.'

He took a puff of his cigarette and added, 'I have myself cased the joint.'

'You have what?'

'Cased the joint.'

My affection and admiration for Buzbee rose to new heights. It was true, then, that he had been moving around and about our town for at least a certain time before making himself known to me. It had indeed been his governmental hat and none other which Mrs Fitzpayne had espied from her terrace. And I saw that his operation of the no-confidence trick upon Harrogate had been enormously facilitated by the fact that Harrogate had indeed seen him lurking about the town on at least two earlier occasions. Things, no doubt, had looked dark enough to Harrogate when he had surmised that Buzbee was no less than a treacherous Irish mercenary in the pay of his rival resort along the coast. How much more appalling for him to be offered grounds for suspicion that Buzbee, Irish or not, was working not for some one-horse outfit seeking to hijack a few thousand tourist pounds, but an authentic commando fighter, perhaps a scarred veteran, in the ranks of the Special Supervisory Tax Detachment. My hopes now rose high. Rapidly summing up the situation I noted:

(1) By driving Harrogate into a nervously defensive position against an obscure but formidable foe, Buzbee had at the worst neutralized him, at the best thrown Harrogate's forces into such disorder that I might take advantage of their confusion to push home my own attack.

(2) Buzbee's quick and percipient appreciation of the state of affairs on the Fitzpayne sector of the front clearly indicated that whatever forces he might be able to mobilize should be brigaded with my own and thrown into the battle.

But here the very consideration which I had mentioned earlier that morning to Irma obtruded itself in ugly fashion. What, I asked myself, was with Edwina Buzbee? What with the irresponsible Pete? Seeing the menace as being in the nature of a bull lumbering thoughtless and sex-crazed across my field of fire, I seized it by the horns.

I might have hesitated to do so had it not been for the increasing certainty that the swaying curtains of rain were not going to be blown at the last moment across the seas to Ireland, but in a few minutes would hit this coast. And a few minutes after that they would hit the hinterland. What then would happen to the Pete-Edwina outing? The weather, inhuman forces, now rushing inland would aid and abet human desire, would topple and sweep away whatever restraint Pete, as an aspiring professional man, as a man with increasing influence among members of the Town Council, as a brother-in-law of myself, might still acknowledge. The sharply lowered visibility, the streaming windscreen, the threat of lightning and the supposed fact that a moving steel vehicle is more likely to attract the thunderbolt than a stationary one; all these would add up to drawing into the side of the road, a sense of intimacy enhanced by supposedly imminent danger of elimination by lightning, the abandonment of those flimsy restraints. As the rain drove darkly from the middle to the near distance my imagination painted for me all too vividly the pull together of those tumescent humans. The awareness of steering wheel and handbrake performing the function of the medieval chastity belt, their placid agreement to transfer themselves to the back seat ('if we are going to have to sit it out we may as well be comfortable'), the first embrace disguised as assistance with the lighting of a cigarette. The quick loosening of clothes (more comfort), the slither of flesh on flesh, the inevitable dénouement.

It seemed to me that the grunts, squeals, and sighs of passion reverberating around the luxurious interior of that mobile gazebo and motorized *Cabinet particulier* must be audible to the ears of Buzbee himself.

I therefore said, 'Now you mention it' (a mistake, since he had not mentioned it) 'your wife seems to have made a big impression on my brother-in-law.' As I thought of the scene about to be enacted in that car I wondered whether 'impres-

sion' would not seem to Buzbee an insultingly ludicrous under-
statement.

'I have noticed it,' he said. 'I have noticed it.' This struck
me as sinister. It could mean that he was preparing either to
pull out or turn nasty at any minute. I raced to create some
kind of diversion.

'I think,' I said, 'it's obviously the result of this strange
accidental resemblance between your wife and mine. Have you
ever,' I asked, still with diversion in mind, 'given much
thought to the question of incest?'

Disregarding this Buzbee said, 'Although when you say
"accidental" I might remark that although the original resemblance was certainly accidental, the bringing together of
these two, their confrontation was not as a matter of fact accidental at all. In fact it was my first sight of your wife when I
was sitting in the car a matter of ten days or so ago opposite
the supermarket which finally tilted my scales; decided me, I
mean, to become a guest in your hotel.'

The rain was now within a few hundred yards of the entrance to the inner bay and with an instinctive movement I
turned up the collar of my jacket. Buzbee looked about for an
ashtray, found it, stubbed out the end of his cigarette and
rose from his seat.

'You follow, of course,' he said, 'my process of thought. In
a relatively strange town there are so many hotels. The field
is to that extent open. And then one observes a man, yourself,
whose face suggests a certain line of thought. He evokes, if
you like, certain memories. One knows, in the course of ordinary chat, that this man is the proprietor of a certain hotel.
Then he (and you must forgive me for saying this but I take it
we are beyond consideration of foolish and deceptive politeness), is advised that the said hotel is hardly of the first class,
pretentious in a certain way but not by any means up to modern
scratch. On a very slightly closer examination of that hotel
one notes to one's genuine, and here I really must underline
the genuineness of genuine, astonishment that the wife of the
proprietor is virtually the double of one's own wife. This dis-

covery is of course decisive. However basically accidental the resemblance, one is going to be provided immediately with a bond of common interest. A fact, which you will appreciate, all to the good.'

'So that was no accident?' I said.

'No accident at all,' said Buzbee. 'And now we must run like hell from the rain.'

With the rain hissing and spitting almost at our heels, we made off across the lawn.

We reached my office, but before I could say anything, before I could even collect my thoughts, Buzbee said, 'It's probably time that I lay my cards on the table. I should tell you a little more about myself. After all, I trust you. And I may say I do so without any thought of whether you in your turn will reciprocate this trust.'

I was about to reply enthusiastically to this offer, when simultaneously with the smash of the rain against my windows, came the ring of the telephone. Mrs Fitzpayne was on the line. She was home, unexpectedly so. Ashleigh had come through.

'In what sense?' I asked in my capacity, both genuinely and strategically, as ardent lover.

'As my tax accountant, what do you think?' said Mrs Fitzpayne. 'If he's right it amounts to an eleven per cent reduction in tax attraction. Isn't that just great?'

'Great enough,' I said, 'and greater still because it brings you home. When will I see you? I mean how many minutes from now?'

'Got the car?' said Mrs Fitzpayne.

'Of course.'

'Fourteen minutes maximum,' said Mrs Fitzpayne. 'Don't fiddle about with that butler, just push the door and walk through the library.'

'You will excuse me,' I said to Buzbee.

'Naturally,' said he.

I made it in rather less than the time estimated by Mrs Fitzpayne, and the immediate result was frankly delicious. And to the pleasures of direct physical sensation succeeded a further state of euphoria in which among the deliciously mingled scents of sweat and tobacco, I relaxed, appraising the situation.

Sixteen

For many days I existed under the influence of another type of happiness. Things were beginning to work out. They were going to work out on all fronts.

In a few days, according to my reckoning, I should be able to inform Harrogate that Mrs Fitzpayne was going to see reason. She was going to decide in favour of obtaining national goodwill and increased financial security in exchange for her residence. At the outset he would naturally maintain his position. He stood for sound finance. That was what the voters voted for when they voted for him. Not a penny on the rates, not for anything.

But then I would give him a shock. The price asked would be so low that even he would have to do some recalculating. And if he thought the news of the price asked might leak to the newspapers, he would have to recalculate even harder. He would begin to wonder whether at that stage it might not be wiser to shift his bet. He could ditch the low-rate voters and pose as public benefactor; the man who got all that real estate for the children, the homeless and the aged.

It occurred to me that, in order to lose no time, it would be desirable that I see him and hint to him what the situation was soon going to be. During that period I visited him several times in his office at the building firm of which he was manager and part owner. His uncertainty could have been pitiful. His moustache ends changed position every few minutes. I had to concentrate on thoughts of his true character to prevent myself feeling sympathy. At first, he tried to find refuge and comfort in the statement that 'if certain eventualities prove concrete, it will be time to take another look at the situation'. Applying pressure by a pincer movement on his left flank, I suggested that it would be possible for damaging rumours to get about. If people heard of Mrs Fitzpayne's likely intentions, and then heard that Harrogate was hostile, or even neutral in the matter, a number of voters might jump to the conclusion that such an attitude could so discourage Mrs Fitzpayne and Westward Ho! Developments, that they would change course, and deprive the citizens of the amenities now almost within reach.

I pointed out how unfortunate it would be for Harrogate if, say, a progressive professional man such as Pete Nordahl were to get that idea, and discuss it with influential members of his clientele. This thrust was given force by the behaviour of sec- retary Eileen, who, to Harrogate's helpless embarrassment, coolly obtruded herself on these conversations. With a lack of diplomacy which made Harrogate squirm, she told me snap- pishly,

'You needn't think you can frighten Harry with that sort of thing. You and your brother-in-law can spread all the rumours you like. Harry will make up his mind in his own time. Harry,' she said, in a phrase evidently learned from American films, 'doesn't scare easily.'

Harrogate was so scared his ulcer began to pain him and he was forced to the indignity of having publicly to gulp down a pill to soothe it. I took care to watch this small operation with close and concerned attention. Eileen sought to counter- attack here by sucking in and puffing out a series of sniffs announcing whisky in the air. I was in no way perturbed. To breathe whisky at Pete Nordahl in the exercise of his medical function was one thing, and a bad one. I felt no such com- punctions about the man Harrogate and Eileen. Let it sicken them. They were the powers of evil. Should my stink discommode them, the worse for them.

Then Eileen said something which caused Harrogate to shake all over inside his clothes.

'And I suppose your friend Mr Buzbee is involved in this,' she said. 'Let me tell you he's a good friend of Harry's. He told Harry only the other day he understood him.'

Harrogate, after the small bout of shakes, said to me:

'He's a great addition to life here. I like him. I'd like to see more of him, if I weren't so busy. Whyn't we all get together one of these early days?'

Eileen said, 'Perhaps Mr Ballanytne isn't so keen on you two getting together. He may have,' she paused to underline it, 'his reasons.'

This thought had Harrogate more scared than ever. Lifting his moustache with two hands he visibly considered whether it might be true that I was in some mysterious manner in league with Buzbee against him, or, alternatively, whether it might be possible to brigade Buzbee with himself against me.

I saw more clearly than before that Buzbee – or rather, Harrogate's fear of Buzbee – was a weapon in my hands. But, as the history of warfare shows, every offensive, if pushed beyond the extent to which its lines of supply are capable of supporting it, may result in a disastrous counter-offensive. In such situations it is necessary to look coolly at the basic factors. And on so doing I at once appreciated the importance of the Pete Nordahl element.

This, somewhat to my disgust, assumed an importance as great as I had declared it to have when I spoke to Irma on the matter of Pete's morning out with Mrs Buzbee. I had hoped that what I said then was a flight of fancy. Now it appeared to me that I had not exaggerated. I made up my mind to deploy available forces on this front, and began by stating the situation to Irma. The phrase 'it is your duty' is often misused. But in this case I felt well-justified in pointing out to Irma that it was her duty to reason together with her brother on this all-important issue. She naturally agreed to do so. And on the following day, as I stood among the shrubs at the top of the path leading down to the pool, I saw them beside the pool, evidently in raging argument.

Since the argument was conducted in Norwegian, all I understood were various oaths uttered by Irma. Oaths are the words one first learns of a foreign language, because they are the phrases most often repeated.

Her voice lowering itself in a menacing manner, Irma went up close to him and, with a fearful Norwegian curse actually snatched off his spectacles. I thought she would then throw them into the pool. Worse than that, she threw them on the ground and crushed them under her foot. Then she rushed at him and with her relatively tiny weight actually threw him backwards into the pool. There he blundered about like a porpoise.

I thought to myself, Is this the persuasive thing to do? Possibly among Norwegians it really is. I decided that in these uncertain circumstances the correct thing was to lie low among the shrubs, playing no role.

I was still there when Irma made her way up from the pool and immediately observed my place of concealment. She said, 'I have done what I can. But you must remember the man is besotted. You had better go speak with him yourself.'

I accosted Pete in his office. And again I had occasion to regret, privately, his lack of a long white coat. Had he been wearing one, I should have felt more confidence in appealing to his professional instincts. I could more freely have pointed out the discrepancy between unbridled, and, above all, public indulgence in sexual sensuality and the requirements of a profession which is also a dedicated public service.

Nevertheless, I pursued my mission. I spoke of his gross irresponsibility. Why, for example, this girl out of all the dozens of girls available? He said (and here I quote him literally), 'Because of all the others girls who, as you rightly say, are available, this is the one I happen to be in love with.'

I found this self-deception shocking, and I told him so. 'What,' I asked him, ' do you mean by love?'

He refused to answer. The more we talked about love the less idea he seemed to have of what is meant by the term. What, I asked him, did he imagine the result would be of his goings-on?

The frivolity and cynicism expressed in his whole attitude were revolting. But at least it made two things clear. First, to argue further with Pete in his present mood was futile. Secondly, the tempo of my own operation must be sharply increased. I must gain my objectives before Pete's activities simultaneously eroded his political influence and in all probability turned Buzbee into a potentially dangerous enemy.

But at this point I suffered an abominable rebuff. In respect of her estate, Mrs Fitzpayne's attitude remained precisely what it had been before our *affaire* began. It influenced her views and inclinations no more than a walk round the bay. She repeated all her former reasons for not taking action – at least not immediately. And she continued to hold frequent telephone conversations with Ashleigh Groom.

Seventeen

It was bitter indeed to realize that one of the situations which I had actually envisaged as a possibility when I was weighing up the pros and cons of undertaking this relationship had in truth come to pass. She really was, it appeared, capable of splitting her personality into two. There was no question that she was enjoying the *affaire*. Nor was there any sign that she was even beginning to weary of it. Yet that made no difference to her attitude in relation to the far more important matter of her property. I had told myself when I was seeking to preview the possibilities that this would amount to a bare-faced swindle. And I had permitted myself to believe her incapable of such an act.

An astonishing feature of the business was that she seemed quite unconscious of acting with lack of scruple. Even after she had, for the third or fourth time, stated her refusal to budge in the matter of the estate, she quite evidently supposed that the *affaire* could continue as before. Worse than useless, obviously, to try to bring her duplicity home to her. However illogically, she would certainly have deluded herself with the idea that it was I who had attempted to take advantage of her, using sex for ulterior motives. That would have meant the final abandonment of my project. And that I refused, even now, to accept. On the other hand I felt myself now quite incapable,

E

in the most physical sense, of carrying on as though she were still the means of carrying the project through.

I was reduced to a humiliating piece of play-acting. We were seated that afternoon in the Colonel's 'library', having a drink before moving to the bedroom as usual. I stood up suddenly, as though to examine a book through the glass of its shelf. To make my action realistic, I actually did peer near and long enough to see the title of this volume which leaned sideways against the four others in the otherwise empty shelf. It was called *Playing the Market – and Keeping Your Shirt*. Then I staggered back a couple of paces, gripping the left side of my chest and giving a small groan. That was supposed to be all. But by misadventure – I think I was a little drunk at the time – I caught my heel on the edge of a rug. Seeking to regain balance, I managed not to fall backwards, but overdid it and fell forward instead. My head, with most of my weight behind it, crashed into and through the flimsy glass of the bookcase. By the time I could thrust myself upright, the book about the stock market was spattered with blood. Blood was also trickling down the side of my face before I could get my handkerchief out to mop it.

The genuine shock resulting from this mishap rendered further play-acting unnecessary. I must have looked, I certainly felt, very much like a man who has suffered a sudden grievous pain in the heart muscle.

With her powerful arms, Mrs Fitzpayne heaved my legs on to the couch. I lay there for a moment with my eyes closed, one hand holding the handkerchief to my cut forehead.

She said, 'Take it easy, just take it easy,' and I heard her striding off to the bathroom where I had often noticed bottles enough to furnish a small chemist's shop. Opening my eyes, I saw her standing above me, watching some pill or powder dissolve in a glass of water. She urged me to drink it down, which I did, although what I actually needed was to drink the rest of my whisky.

I finished the water with the pill in it, and began to mutter something about 'getting these attacks occasionally. Nothing to worry about.'

To my surprise she said, ' Naturally there's nothing to worry about. An awful lot of people get them every once in a while. Used to happen to a friend of George that worked in our American State Department. It's just . . .' But I was unable to catch the term she used, obviously a medical term of some kind. This I regretted, because in the hurry of staging my act I had given no thought to defining exactly what it was that was supposed to ail me. I asked what had happened to the man from the State Department. She said he had had to take it very very easy for a week or two.

I concentrated on the thought that the first thing to do after such a seizure was to ' take things very easy '. This would at least facilitate the concealment of my physical impotence occasioned by the shocking disillusionment I had suffered as a result of her social non-cooperation. She told me I should rest for a little while. After the first shock of falling into the bookcase, I had no need of rest. But I did have need of contemplation. Feigning exhaustion, I closed my eyes again and contemplated vigorously. At the end of approximately ten minutes I had reached a fairly obvious conclusion. The time had come to mobilize Buzbee.

So that when Mrs Fitzpayne suggested she drive me into town I first said I would prefer to walk as usual. She of course said that walking was contra-indicated for a man in my condition. Then I said that it would be embarrassing for me to arrive at my hotel in her car, at five in the afternoon, with a noticeable gash in my forehead. I certainly did not, I told her, want the whole town to know that I was subject to these occasional seizures. That would be bad for trade, bad for credit. Who wants to stay in an hotel where the proprietor is liable to fall flat on his face in the middle of a tourist-type conversation about the local amenities and beauty spots? And if people were told nothing of the seizure they would assume that I had fallen down drunk, which, too, could be somewhat bad for me and worse for her. How did it happen, they were going to ask, that this man was out there at Mrs Fitzpayne's house in mid-afternoon and presently became so drunk he fell down and cut himself? I said I had a better idea. I would simply telephone a good friend who would drive out and pick me up.

She was going to say, 'But,' and had just got as far as saying it when I said, 'A very discreet friend. Mr Buzbee's a man who knows how to keep his mouth shut.'

She said, 'My God! that Government man,' and I said, 'I don't know whether he's a Government man or not. So far as I know he's just a man on holiday. You shouldn't be so suspicious.'

'We'd better get on down to the drawing-room and look like respectable citizens,' said Mrs Fitzpayne as I rang off. When we got there she said, 'I just don't like to have that man in the house. I told you before, he's a Governmental type. How do I know he isn't casing the joint?'

Just for a moment I was checked in thought by recollection of Buzbee's own use of the phrase in connection, precisely, with Mrs Fitzpayne's house. Mrs Fitzpayne, abnormally sensitive in such matters, pounced sharply.

'Why are you looking like that?' she said. 'You think he really may be casing the joint? What's the matter?'

I said, 'You mean you think he's a potential burglar?'

She told me not to be a damn fool. 'Burglars I can stand for,' she said. 'What've I got to lose that they can take away in a van? Two vans? I mean casing it for the Government, the tax people.'

I said, 'But what possible reason can you have for supposing such a thing?'

She said, 'Well, because,' and then the butler announced 'Mr Buzbee.'

For just a minute I thought it must be by some kind of miracle that Buzbee, arriving just then, looked as he did. Naturally he was carrying no brief-case, and had left his hat in the hall. Yet he perfectly conveyed the impression of a man who is carrying a Civil Service type of brief-case and is wearing what Mrs Fitzpayne had called a 'Governmental hat'. And although his clothes were those in which I had often seen him, they made an impression of being in some not easily defined way insufficiently brushed. Such was the power of his personality that one could believe that the seat of his trousers might be a little bit shiny from sitting in some chair in Whitehall, cold-bloodedly plotting the ensnarement and downfall of such as Mrs Fitzpayne.

I almost immediately grasped that this was no miracle. This was Buzbee, my ally, who had exactly calculated the expectations and fears of Mrs Fitzpayne and was here to give added reality to them both.

She offered him a drink with that small excess of eagerness with which a person with a guilty conscience offers a drink to a visiting policeman. And he, at once noting that she was already slightly off-balance, accepted it after a tiny hesitation in which one felt he might easily have said, 'Not while on duty, thank you,' but had decided that, just for the moment, he was not on duty.

There we sat in the sunshine, and the notion came to me that, in a sufficiently bizarre fashion, the sunshine itself was on Buzbee's side. In the sense, I mean, that it shed lustre on the whole magnificent lay-out, interior and exterior; pointing out the grandeur, the huge tax-worthiness of the great apartment and its furnishings, and connecting these with the equal grandeur of the lawn (a greensward if ever I saw one), and the great trees beyond. And it could be seen that Buzbee's eyes, in a quiet, routine, but not quite on-duty manner, were taking note of all these things, the movement of his eyes seeming more important than the strictly trivial and conventional remarks uttered through his lips. The impression was given that even if he did not know exactly where the body was buried, he knew there was a body buried somewhere, and thus could afford time to go through the motions of polite conversation.

Feeling herself and her whole possessions subjected to this terrible scrutiny, Mrs Fitzpayne became – it was the phrase that occurred to me – mentally muscle-bound. While Buzbee made quiet enquiries about my health, and commented on the fineness of the afternoon, her manner made evident that she considered these remarks a mere smoke screen. In other words, she was already in the position of a person who knows that there is a body on the premises, and knows that the supposedly off-duty policeman knows it too. The more commonplace and innocuous Buzbee's remarks, the more sinister they obviously seemed to her.

From being no more than a little off-balance she became absolutely rattled. Like a body-burier whose tension is such that after a while he has to talk about the burying of bodies, Mrs Fitzpayne – quite unprompted by Buzbee – started to talk about the cost of living in Britain, the high rate of taxation. Buzbee said he supposed taxation was pretty high everywhere. He had the air of a man to whom the question of taxation, its comparative incidence and so on, is of no less, but certainly of no more interest than the question, for instance, of whether the weather forecasters are usually correct, or the extent to which the compulsory instalment of safety belts might reduce fatalities in motor-car accidents.

This pose, as she considered it to be, set Mrs Fitzpayne's nerves jangling. She mixed herself a dry martini and then, in a fatal self-revelation, with great deliberation set it down on the table without so much as sipping it. Anyone could see, and certainly Buzbee could see, that while the desire for another drink was natural, the sudden act of refraining from it was a disclosure of a state of mind – the drawing of a map. It said, 'My God I need a drink. But my God! I mustn't let this man see I need it.' From which it was easy to proceed to the question of just why she needed it so badly, and why she needed so badly to conceal that she needed it. Not taking the drink was a confession that the burial place of the body was not well concealed.

Buzbee rather ostentatiously finished his drink, gave a solicitous look at me, and turned to Mrs Fitzpayne. His manner was that of a guest who fears that he has perhaps shown insufficient interest in the hobby of his host or hostess. She might have been talking about stamp collecting or Japanese rock gardens. He said, getting up at the same time, 'That's very interesting indeed, Mrs Fitzpayne. I can see there's a lot more to this tax business than the layman is apt to think. By the way,' he said to her, offering me the succouring hand of a friend to invalid friend to help me from my seat, 'our friend here told me you know a man called Ashleigh Groom. *He's* something in the tax line isn't he?'

'You know Ashleigh?'

'Not really to say "know",' said Buzbee. 'Just to shake the hand a couple of times at a party here and there. He wouldn't know me. But I know a number of people who know him.'

As she stood on the steps to see us off, her bright smile was as revealing of tension as had been her rejection of the martini.

'It may seem a little early to say so,' Buzbee said as we drove down the avenue, 'but I think we may already be at the end of the beginning.'

And so indeed it seemed. It became more and more obvious to me in the days that followed that Buzbee, after that first encounter, was daily increasing his leverage, if I may so put it, on Mrs Fitzpayne. Daily, I gather – partly from herself, partly from Buzbee – her conviction of the power of the SSTD increased. Daily diminished, accordingly, the malign influence of Ashleigh Groom. Telephonic consultations between Mrs Fitzpayne and Buzbee sometimes seemed almost continuous. And almost daily her car was at the door of the hotel to carry off Buzbee for conversations deemed too intimate to be conducted over the telephone.

Eighteen

It would be desirable at this point to quote in some detail from my diary of the days that followed, all of them happy ones for me. But I find that many, many pages of that diary are missing. And I recall, though not quite clearly, that at some catastrophic later point when despair temporarily succeeded hope, I tore out those pages which seemed to me to expose my hopes too crudely. They exposed me, I thought, as a fool.

The pages that remain do, however, tell something of my experiences during those days and weeks. I speak of the period during which I supposed that all was going well.

I copied into my diary relevant extracts from newspapers and magazines, bearing on the problems of the children and the homeless. I noted 'It is for the first time possible for me to assemble all these facts together, and calmly survey the whole horrible picture they compose. Why have I not done this before? Because I could not face both the facts themselves and the likelihood that nothing whatever could after all be done to change them. Now with the possibility, the probability, of a major move forward, the facts become tolerable.'

To this statement which, the moment I had written it, looked to me somewhat high-coloured, I added a further note. 'It occurs to me that it is for another reason that I find it possible to face the facts now. This reason concerns the facts less than it does myself. That is to say that until now I have suffered long periods not only of discouragement but of absolute lack of confidence in my own judgement and abilities. I have been oppressed by visions of total failure due to weaknesses in myself. NOW all that is altered. Now I have absolute confidence. ALL WILL BE WELL.'

Although there is no reference in the diary, I recall that it was on that same day that, for the first time in a good many weeks I patrolled the poor quarters of the town re-visiting streets, alleys and courts which were the loathsome physical facts upon which the articles and statistics and reports of debates in the Town Council were based. I talked with some of the victims of these conditions. I encountered briefly the parents of the two children who had played at Buddhist priests. They were out of hospital and, it seemed, in good health. Their mother's attitude was discouraged and discouraging. Her voice and general deportment were that of a woman worn out with toil and care. She took the view that the whole episode had been the fault of the children. She had picked up the word 'delinquent' and applied it to them repeatedly. It occurred to me that in the Middle Ages she would perhaps have said that they were possessed of the Devil. When I tried to suggest that the housing conditions under which they lived (the whole family shared two rooms with another family of three) might be responsible, she took violent offence, as though I were accusing her, as a housewife, of somehow being responsible for the children's behaviour.

She looked at me with hate, and in a tired snarl announced astonishingly: 'Kids nowadays have it too good. Think they can run wild. Don't you read the papers? Delinquents, that's what they are.'

Her husband also had an air of being defeated, and stood by saying nothing during this conversation. But later he walked a little way with me down the street to the corner pub. There rancour trickled from him. But it was directed not against the children or delinquency but against the Government and the Town Council. As a couple of pints of beer furnished him

E*
137

energy, he extended his range of fire. He included the world oil interests responsible for despatching the giant tanker which had originally spilled the oil on to our beaches. In the crazy rush to save time and money the skipper of the tanker had been forced on to a dangerous course at too high a speed. 'Don't you know that?' he asked me with a sneer in his voice. 'I know it and you know it and everyone in this town knows it. And what happens? Nothing. And why?' He was back again to the Government and the Town Council. It amounted, he said, to a conspiracy.

To my mind his view was basically sound. Sounder at any rate than that of his poor wife. I remember regretting only that misfortune or overwork had so debilitated him that even his indignation was a feeble thing.

I felt the need to give him, as the saying goes, a shot in the arm, something to restore him to confidence and hope. I told him he could take it from me that big changes were coming in our town. He deliberately let off a loud fart, spat on the floor, and farted again. It was evidently a comment he could utter at will.

I told him, as cheerfully as I could, that changes really were coming. As I paid for the last round of drinks I saw his face in the mirror behind the bar. His expression was one of cynical contempt.

As I quit the pub and walked briskly towards the hotel I felt suddenly uneasy. It was as though a cold shadow had suddenly fallen across the sunshine of my mood of hope and confidence. I remember that for a moment I stood quite still on the pavement, concentrating. Had I over-estimated the favourable factors in the situation? Were there lurking somewhere unfavourable ones which I had overlooked? I could think of none. So why, I asked myself, the falling of this sudden shadow, like what people used to call a premonition? Then in a flash I seemed to have the answer. In the pub, for obvious reasons of courtesy, I had drunk beer, my companion's choice, rather than whisky. I detest beer, and it affects my stomach like soapy water. Clearly it was this liquid chill on the stomach which had produced that moment of uneasiness. Hastening my steps to the hotel, I reached my office and quickly downed a couple of strong whiskies. The effect was almost immediate. Hope and confidence returned. I remember laughing to myself at the thought that even in rational persons an unexplained queasiness, produced by such an ordinary cause as two or three pints of beer, could give rise to irrational fears and belief in premonitions of ill fortune.

Much relieved and restored in spirits I found myself singing aloud a couple of verses from the *Battle Hymn of The Republic*. And after lunch and a nap, the day (July 4) being warm and sparkling, I reflected that for most of this summer I had felt myself too busy, too engaged in my projects, ever to take advantage of the amenities offered by our seashore and countryside. All this loveliness, out there beyond the bungalows and the filling stations, was available to be enjoyed, a means of maintaining and extending one's capacity for appreciation. I was more than usually aware of the swift turning of our planet and of the process of personal physical decay. It may be deemed fanciful to say that I felt as though a window or curtain had opened somewhere and through it a clear voice was summoning me to go for a spin in the country. I obeyed that voice.

I drove on along the lower sea road for twenty-five miles or so until the westering sun shining from almost directly in front made proper appreciation of the landscape difficult. I turned north, inland, crossing the main east-west road into the hinterland of steepish slopes and wide valleys. Everything was a delight to the eye. And as I crossed ridge after ridge I more and more felt that I was moving into enchanted country. Each ridge behind me seemed a guarantee, as it were, of some sort of seclusion and security.

Topping one higher than the rest I saw in front of me a green valley with a brown stream sparkling along it. Beside a stone bridge stood what evidently had once been an unusually large farmhouse, also of stone. But I could see, just this side of the bridge, a sign swung between two poles. I could read the word 'Inn' but not the name. I experienced quite sharply the feeling that the whole valley with its inn had just been created for my benefit, to delight and welcome me. I remember that this fancy was so strong that I carefully checked my mileage, with the notion that I must know as exactly as possible where I was in case at some later time the place vanished.

I drove gently down to the stream. The sign said Valley Inn. I turned into the first opening I saw in the grey wall of the inn and found myself in a farmyard, surrounded on three sides by farm outbuildings. There was no other vehicle in the yard except a tractor just visible under the roof of the shed. I saw that this was not, as I had supposed, the front of the inn but its back premises. Not bothering to take the car on to the road again and circle the building, I went across the yard to where, at the top of three stone steps, a door stood open. A roughly stone-flagged passage led towards the front of the house past an open door through which I could see the corner of what seemed a spacious farmhouse kitchen. Then there was a doorway with no door, and beyond that the passage broadened to four or five times its width, to the size of a room, and there were rugs covering the stone. From a glance at the layout I could see that this must be the front hall or lobby of the Valley Inn. My eye was caught by the familiar sight of a standard type of visitors' book lying open on a high oak table. With the natural interest of a man in the hotel business, I walked across to examine it. I wanted to know what sort of business an inn did in an enchanted valley. Not much, apparently. Probably the owners supported themselves mainly by working the farm. In fact during the past week only two guests had registered. The only entry during that period was for a Mr and Mrs Leeds who had checked in the day before.

I was looking about for a smoke room or bar when a door on the left opened and a young woman went past me to the open front door. Standing in a small glazed-in porch she called out into the open air for Mrs Leeds. There was an unintelligible answering call from outside. The young woman raised her voice to shout 'Your tea's ready.' On her return I asked her where I should go to get a drink, if it was not too early. It was just after half past five but I thought that here the opening hours might be other than our own and did not want to embarrass the innkeepers. She said it was certainly not too early and pointed to a door on the other side of the lobby. As I strolled towards it I glanced out of the front door and saw Edwina Buzbee coming across the porch. I greeted her warmly, and without surprise. There could be a dozen reasons why she and Buzbee should call themselves Mr and Mrs Leeds. Nothing Buzbee might choose to do in that way surprised me. I said to Edwina it was fun meeting them there, and was going to invite them to a drink when they had finished their tea when Pete Nordahl came into the porch behind her.

Much as I deplored, and for good reason, Pete's indiscreet association with Edwina, I felt that his presence here with the Buzbees was a healthy sign. Reason, it could seem, had prevailed and Pete was now content to join them in the capacity of good friend. I paid a mental tribute to what I felt must have been Buzbee's particularly skilful treatment of dangerously hot-headed, irresponsible Pete. In these circumstances I greeted him with a warm wave of the hand.

'Where's Norman?' I said. 'Isn't he coming in to tea?'

'He's not here,' Pete said.

'Gone back to town already on an afternoon like this?' I said. I felt contrite. No doubt it was activity on behalf of myself and my plans which had taken him back. I said 'He works too hard.'

Pete looked me harshly in the eye and said, 'He hasn't *gone back* to town. He hasn't been here at all.' And Edwina said in an odd voice, as though she were registering relief of some kind, 'He doesn't know where this is. He couldn't find it if he tried.'

I suffered what I can only describe as a rictus or spasm. I did not have to take in, as they say, still less to consider what the brutal consequences of this brutish behaviour could be. Full realization of them exploded in my head like a load of plastique. One second I was standing rigid, the next I felt myself thrown forward as though by some outside explosive force. I was hurled towards Pete like a projectile. He staggered back and sideways against the wall of the porch. My fist, again as though it were independently propelled, went straight for the bridge of his nose, base of his spectacles, which were torn from it and sent flying. As my body weight hit him, the impact drove him slithering along the porch wall. As he thus eluded me I saw that the porch was not on a level with the gravel of the small driveway leading to it. There were two steep steps of the old-fashioned farmhouse type. As he fell, he took the force of them on his shoulders and backside, his head landing lightly enough on the gravel. Still, he was momentarily stunned. And as I looked down at him I felt that the explosive charge which had shot me at him was exhausted.

After a couple of seconds he got to his feet and started to come groggily up the steps. He steadied himself and lashed out at me, almost literally blindly. Edwina pushed violently past me and caught him, holding on with both hands.

'Not here. Not now,' she said.

'Find my glasses,' Pete said hoarsely. 'I'm going to give him hell.'

Edwina continued clinging to his arm. 'No, no,' she said with anguish in her voice. 'I'll get your glasses but don't fight him. Not now, not here. There'll be noise, people will come. There'll be a scandal here in the inn.'

Pete stood there blinking and growling in his throat.

'Be a scandal anyway when I go for him, here or wherever.'

Edwina was sobbing. 'But not *here*,' she said. 'We couldn't stay on tonight and we'd never get to come back here. I don't *want*,' she said piteously, 'to be turned out of here.'

Pete fetched a deep breath. 'All right,' he said. 'I suppose I understand. But for God's sake get those glasses.'

Before she could do so I had myself jumped down the steps and found the glasses which I then handed to him. We stood glaring at one another. Edwina looked from one to other of us. Her whole face trembled with anxiety lest, it seemed, they be thrown out of their temporary garden of Eden for creating a disturbance. She seemed to make some sort of decision and, concentrating on Pete, pleaded with him.

'We'd better explain everything,' she said. 'James doesn't understand a thing.'

'You're damn right he doesn't,' said Pete. 'So why doesn't he keep his bloody snout out?' He cursed in Norwegian.

She was looking at me with cold fury, but what she said was, 'We have to explain the situation. Otherwise anything can happen.' She swallowed. 'I'm so tired of trouble,' she said plaintively.

'In that case,' said Pete, looking past my head instead of at me, 'I suppose you'd better join us at our high tea.'

The idea of, in the frightful circumstances, sitting down to tea and eggs and bacon and sausages at quarter to six in the afternoon revolted me. I may say that at my age the notion of high tea revolts me at the best of times. This is because it recalls to me a period of my life when I could not afford any other sort of meal in the evening, and was always forced to drink tea or cocoa rather than wine. Mention of high tea, its physical presence, has the effect of suggesting to me that such a period might quite easily recur. It is a symbol of misfortune.

My hesitation, misinterpreted by Pete who could not know just what high tea meant to me, brought about a return of his belligerence.

'You see. He doesn't *want* an explanation,' he said to Edwina.

I wondered whether it would be desirable in the interests of general calmness and understanding to set forth in full my feelings about high tea. I decided against it. I said instead, 'It's just that I need a little while to calm down. Also in the tea-room or whatever they call it there'll be a maid, lurking and eavesdropping. Afterwards you can join me in the bar. I'll find a quiet corner.'

By the time Pete and Edwina came in, I had just finished my first drink. They asked for gin and tonic and I sat by the window drinking silently for a frozen moment. Then Pete said, 'The situation is that Edwina is going to leave your Mr Buzbee. I'm going to marry her.'

Speaking through a sharp pain in my chest, I said dully to Edwina in order to say something, 'You're divorcing him? Or you'll let him divorce you?'

Edwina and Pete spoke simultaneously. 'Neither,' they said. Edwina said, 'It won't be necessary. We're not married.'

Nineteen

I held myself awfully still. There came into my mind memory of a chess tournament I had once played in. At that time I was reckoned a player with great potentialities. I might be selected to play for the County, which would very much have strengthened my position at that school I then taught at. In this particular game, upon the result of which a great deal depended, I had developed my attack with a good deal more than my normal skill. I was, in fact, at the top of my form. My opponent was rattled, beginning to make foolish moves. My victory seemed nearly assured. At that point, some lout who was looking on, reached greedily to snatch a glass from a tray of drinks being carried by the steward of the little club where the match was taking place. In doing so he stumbled against our table, rocked it, and sent the chessboard slithering to the floor. We had to re-start the game. But the shock, disappointment and disgust had drained me of mental energy. I lost humiliatingly.

Was it possible that the careless and callous lusts of this young couple, Pete and Edwina, were at this late stage in my present game going to be allowed to upset the entire chessboard?

I heard myself say in a voice which sounded strange even to myself, ' Impossible.'

'Nothing impossible about it,' Pete said in a calm tone which nearly maddened me. 'A fact.'

I could believe that this girl Edwina of whom I knew almost nothing and who might, for all I knew, be ignorant of the most important factors in the situation, might act in this devastating manner. But surely not Pete? A detestable inner voice whispered to me, 'Well, why not Pete?' I disregarded it.

'Pete,' I said to him, almost turning my back on the girl. 'You know the facts. You know Buzbee's part, his quite essential part in my plans for the town, for the general future? You know what can happen, what almost damn certainly will happen if you go ahead the way you're going? He'll pull out in a spirit of mortification and hatred.'

Pete shrugged, and at that I must have looked as though I were going to hit him again, for he leaned back in his chair and gripped his glass.

'As I told you,' I said, keeping my voice as low and even as possible, 'your mere – what shall I say? – *liaison* or flirtation with this young woman was bad enough, dangerous enough. And this,' I made a gesture indicating the whole locale of the Valley Inn where we sat, 'this, coming here as man and wife, is carrying things to the point of madness. But your present proposal . . .' The enormity of it nearly choked me and I had to break off to take a pull at my whisky.

'There's nothing you can say or do about it, Jim,' said Pete. Edwina nodded and seemed to be giving him a secret smile. I turned on her in restrained indignation.

'I hope,' I said bitterly, 'you are proud of your part in this. Let me say right away that I am making no criticism at all of the fact that you are not married to Buzbee. There may be a dozen good reasons for that. In fact, I reckoned with that at the outset. A harmless deception. But you were guilty of another deception which was by no means harmless.'

'And what was that?' Pete asked threateningly.

'You gave the impression,' I said, continuing to speak to Edwina, 'that you loved and cherished Buzbee as he obviously loves and cherishes you. Admittedly, given your relative ages, it was an unusual association. But that very fact implies,' I said vehemently, 'it implies the existence of more than usually powerful bonds of love and affection. It was natural for me to assume that. And now it would appear that you were misleading us all along and that you are prepared to cast off Buzbee like an old shoe.'

'You don't understand,' Pete growled. But I kept on talking to the girl. I asked how old she was and she said she was nineteen. And how long had she been living with Buzbee? A little over a year.

'There you are,' I said. 'Your feeling for Buzbee is such that it has overcome conventional prejudices as to age. That very, very deep feeling has persisted for more than a year. I admit that Pete here is a good-looking young fellow. But surely you must see that your feeling for him is unlikely to be more than a damn fleeting fancy compared to the depth of your feeling for Buzbee? And yet for this fleeting fancy, this casual whim you are prepared not only to break Buzbee's heart, ruin his life for all I know, but also . . .'

Despite gestures and ejaculated interruptions from Pete I continued sternly on my course, pointing out to her as I had to Pete at the outset, the consequences of her action in an area much larger than the purely personal.

'If you only knew,' I was saying, 'the background of these children I am speaking of,' when she abruptly broke in.

'And what,' she said, 'about *my* background?'

That dismaying conversation remains horribly vivid in my mind.

Myself: What background? When?

Edwina: I mean the way I was living before the court action. Before he had to change his way of life and skip out of town.

Myself: What action? What town?

Edwina: The action where the Judge as good as declared him guilty as a solicitor of embezzling clients' funds. The Judge's only regret was that due to his agile manipulations there wasn't enough evidence to convict him along with some of his associates. That was in Glasgow eighteen months ago. I daresay the case didn't get reported down here. Buzbee's name was Bronterre then. He had to change it.

Myself: I never heard of the case. And anyway what had it to do with you?

Edwina: My father used to do little piddling jobs for Buzbee. Sometimes when he had to go to Buzbee's office he used to take me with him.

Myself: And that was how you fell in love with one another?

Edwina: It wasn't quite like that. My father was a shabby little man who drank most of the little money he ever earned. We lived in more or less a slum.

Myself: Couldn't you get away on your own? Couldn't you get a job?

Edwina: I did have several jobs. But father would take the money off me before I had a chance to move from our place and later, when I wouldn't give it him, he'd find out where I was working and come down and make scenes and I'd get the sack.

Myself: And Buzbee?

Edwina: Buzbee said to me one day after the court action that we were both what he called orphans of the storm. He said we should throw in our lot together.

Myself: You mean he offered to marry you?

Edwina: How could he? He was married. It was only just after the case that his wife left him and started to divorce him. She had all sorts of grounds. Of course her leaving made him feel lonely.

Myself: So you agreed to live with him?

Edwina: Natural enough, wasn't it, considering the way I was fixed?

Myself: Well yes. One can't deny that.

Edwina: Besides, Buzbee offered my father quite a nice sum to get him to help persuade me. It just meant that my father bullied me more than ever to accept Buzbee's offer.

Myself: And you didn't then or later have any feeling for Buzbee at all?

Edwina: Not exactly in the way you mean, I suppose.

Myself: But with your looks there must have been plenty of more suitable men who'd have married you.

Edwina: Some of them didn't want to marry me, and in that time before I met Buzbee I was in such a horror of the kind of life I had to lead that finally I got the horrors at the idea of marrying anyone that wasn't really rich and secure. I was afraid my sort of life would go on for ever, except I'd have a husband instead of a father.

Myself: But later. After you lived with Buzbee. You must have met a richer sort of man. Where did you live?

Edwina: We travelled about. And you see by that time what I felt about Buzbee was that he was my security. That was the most important thing I wanted. And if a man gives you the most important thing you want well then the way you feel for him is the same as love. I mean, you won't understand this, but if what you most want is security and he gives it you you don't think 'I don't love this man but I'll live with him because I want security.' The two things kind of melt together. It's the same as love.

Myself: Even . . .

Pete: Oh, for God's sake, lay off.

Edwina: Even when it comes to sex? Yes, I'd say it is. You see a girl marry an ugly old millionaire and you think she's saying to herself, 'I can't bear the sight of the old gargoyle, but I'll go through with it for the sake of the money.' But I don't think that's so. I think the money makes them actually love him. Makes them sexy, anyway.

Pete: I don't think I'm standing for this.

Edwina: Be quiet, Pete. I want him to understand.

Myself: So you travelled lovingly about.

Pete: Another crack like that and . . .

Edwina: Of course he'd made quite a lot of money out of whatever it was the Judge said he'd done but couldn't get him for. He was looking for an outlet. What he called an area of operation.

Myself: And this was it?

Edwina: Not at once. We travelled all over.

Myself: So why here, now?

Edwina: We were some place in East Anglia, or it could have been Bristol, and he saw this what they call a brochure about this place here. In colour. Issued by the Town Council or the Regional Council or the County Council or some damn Council. You know the way it is.

Myself: I do indeed. Proceed.

Edwina: Well the set-up as described caught his eye. What it amounted to was, and I think he told me this, that what they had there was a community which was pretty well-to-do but not too much so. He didn't want to go some place where there wasn't any money at all. Other hand, he wouldn't want to be in a pool along with the big sharks. He couldn't have handled them, not given the handicaps he was under on account of that case in Glasgow.

Myself: And on coming here he found the place lived up to his expectations?

Edwina: Obviously. It was just what that brochure said it was. Just for instance, there was only that one really big rich house – your Mrs Fitzpayne's. And the rest of the layout seemed to be what he called what the doctor ordered.

Myself: But what made him come to my hotel?

Edwina: A chance, an accident. He saw Irma in the street. He saw at once that she was my double. He found out she was the wife of a man who kept an hotel and so he went to that hotel. He said it was a sign.

Myself: Sign of what? From whom?

Edwina: God, I suppose, or something of the kind. He's extremely superstitious. It's his form of religion I suppose you could say. I've heard lots of crooks are religious or superstitious or whatever you want to call it. Also he said there aren't such things as accidents.

Myself: But this was one. What else?

Edwina: Still, you could see how it seemed to him to mean something.

Myself: And of course that brought Pete into it. I mean he

had this feeling for Irma and then you come along. What a signpost Norman picked.

Pete: It happened. What's it matter how it happened? Everything's going to be different from now on.

Myself: But can't you postpone everything a bit? Just until my project's got through?

Edwina: I'm not going back to him even for a day.

Myself: But he'll blow up. He'll leave town. He'll drop the whole thing.

Pete: Best thing that could happen to you. He's a crook. He's a con-man.

Because I remember Pete urging me to lower my voice, I suppose I must have nearly shouted under the frightful strain of this crisis. Thoughts, arguments, apprehensions of disaster, hopes half dead but still alive and struggling, seemed to be fighting to get hold of some effective words and beat down all opposition. I sought to explain to them that, admitting Buzbee might be a crook in the wide, more or less abstract sense, pertaining, moreover, to the past, in this particular state of affairs, this here and now, he was a positive force for goodness, honesty and general improvement. In fact, I said, his very crookedness was working on the right side. It was arguable I said, that his whole life and training as a con-man had been a necessary preparation for his mastery of Mrs Fitzpayne, resulting, if Pete and Edwina would only not wreck the whole design, in immense benefit to our community.

Pete interrupted to ask nastily whether I implied that God had guided him to swindle people in Glasgow and all over just so that he would be in good training to deal with Mrs Fitzpayne? And then he said again, 'And for God's sake don't shout. Don't make a scene. We want to stay here.' And Edwina put her hand on my arm and said, 'Yes, please, please.'

Things were a little misty. The strain and excitement had driven the whisky to my head, as the saying goes. But I could see their faces well enough and hear their voices saying those things, and I suddenly knew there was nothing to be done about them. Theirs was a hopeless case. I remember saying to them several times, 'Yours is a hopeless case.' They were, I told them, in the the fullest sense anti-social.

I was aware of urgency, of the need for something to be done immediately. It was my intention to walk straight out of that place and drive back to town in order to take some action the nature of which I would determine *en route*. It occurred to me, however, that nothing could be more harmful to my cause than for me to be summoned for allegedly drunken driving. Caution was desirable. The delay involved was exasperating. In consequence I did not hesitate to address this precious pair with some violence.

'I need,' I said, 'an hour's sleep. I shall take it on two chairs in this bar. You, I make no doubt, are only too anxious to withdraw to the bed which you have reserved.'

Pete started to say something, but Edwina patted him in turn on the sleeve and said, 'Please, please,' to him, and they took themselves off. Just before they did so, Edwina, already on her feet, said to me:

'I could tell you one little thing about Norman Buzbee that might give you a better idea than anything else how deceptive he is.'

I asked her 'What?' and she annoyingly said, 'No, you'll have to take my word for it. It was the only thing he trusted me about, I think. Also it was something I could only have found out in bed.'

Pete snarled from behind her and they went.

Sleep, while steadying my nerves, left me a little muzzy in the head. A final large whisky cured that, and I drove fast but impeccably into town. As I drove, I determined that the wisest course was immediately to seek out Buzbee and, before he could learn of Edwina's seduction by my sex-crazed brother-in-law, confront him with some new factors in the situation calling for rapid acceleration of action on the Fitzpayne front. She must, if necessary, be crudely presented with the probability of devastating action by the taxation authorities unless she made haste to divest herself of her principal English possession, her house, and offer it in written and irrevocable form to the town. I meditated on the nature of the 'new factors' which might be supposed to have arisen during the last twenty-four hours or so.

These meditations proved futile. Irma, greeting me in the hotel garden, informed me that both Buzbee and Mrs Fitzpayne were still in London on business. Buzbee had telephoned to the hotel saying that he was not to be expected until the following day at the earliest.

'And so what,' Irma said, holding me by the hand and looking at me, 'seems to be the matter?'

With sixty-six varieties of roses blooming all around us – I knew that there were that many because Irma had told me so – I told her of the latest developments culminating at the Valley Inn. But as I did so I felt a good deal in need of the fullest possible confidence on the part of Irma. I had felt that need often and over many years, but rarely so acutely as now. Therefore, although I was not such a fool as to suppose it would come as any sort of news to her, I for the first time candidly and fully charted for her the course of my relationship with Mrs Fitzpayne.

'That's of course,' she said, still holding my hand with one of hers and snapping off the top of a dead plant with the other. 'In such a conjecture we must bend our thoughts upon the first Duke of Marlborough, noted in history and legend for his use of sex in the interests of his country. So it said in our Norwegian history books. And because,' she said, turning from me a little to bend and peer into the heart of a rose, 'our teachers were Puritan in tendency the suggestion was that in order to advance himself to the highest positions to do the most good, he forced himself to sleep with harridans, with hags, with utter old bags. *Per ardua ad astra* was the theme. But I daresay were truth told many of them were quite dishes. Norah Fitzpayne's a dish, as nobody can deny.'

'I deny nothing,' I said.

She abandoned her examination of the rose and peered closely at me instead.

'And now,' she said, 'clutching at your entrails like the

clammy half-human paw of a primitive missing link, is the thought that my acceptance of the situation, my speedy thumbs-up, is but the result of indifference towards you, not of good sense. You are thinking perhaps that after all there may have been a little something more than met your beaming eye in my relations with my loving brother Peter.'

Since that very thought had in fact at that moment scuttered across my mind, I had to hesitate while I took a closer look at it and rejected it with contumely.

'So,' she said, 'between the nod of one rose and the next your heart arraigns me of frigidity, incest and more if you had time to read over the catalogue, you stertorous toad-thing. But you know and I know,' she said, gently pulling me down on to a patch of soft grass where the rose bushes were widely spaced, 'that I'm no more indifferent to you than I am to,' she looked around, 'to this garden. I couldn't say fairer than that, could I?'

That, I knew, was indeed the case. The resultant sense of elation was such that it was a considerable time before I realized that noises of which I had been scarcely aware were coming from the road, a hundred yards or so above us. Youths, it seemed, had found some vantage point on the wall from which they could play Peeping Tom with our rose garden. Of this they were taking full advantage. They whistled and ululated. They gave out shrill cries of sexual encouragement. But when at length I raised myself on an elbow and turned my head to look at them I saw that two out of the five were standing motionless and apparently silent, gazing down on us, one could only suppose, with the wide-eyed insatiable stare of the voyeur.

'Let us hope,' said Irma, reclining with her arms behind her head, 'that they too have loved ones to whom they can now make hot haste.'

Twenty

Each day for three days I telephoned the butler at the Fitz-payne house. Each day it was announced that they were ex-pected 'tomorrow'. On that first evening of my return from my excursion to the Valley Inn Irma had said to me that she supposed I realized that not only the utility but the very ex-istence of my *affaire* with Norah Fitzpayne was at an end. I said that of course I had. 'That Buzbee,' she said, 'has moved in on the ground floor.'

This observation surprised me. I had seen Buzbee in the light of her, so to speak, spiritual mentor, advising, admonish-ing and where necessary threatening her, all with the general objective of snatching her from the grip of the man Groom and guiding her in the direction in which, in my well-con-sidered opinion, she should go. I had not thought of him as her lover. 'But to me,' said Irma, 'it has for a long time been sticking out a kilometre, viz five-eighths of a mile. You'll see.'

And on the fourth day I did. I had grown tired of telephon-ing the butler, only to learn of further postponements of the return. I had begun to feel these calls to be obscurely humiliat-ing, suggesting perhaps to the butler that I was in a bad way and could scarcely live without the presence of the absent pair. But on the afternoon of that day Buzbee telephoned to me from the Fitzpayne house. He had gone there direct, without stopping to leave his baggage at the hotel.

After very brief mutual greetings he asked me could I come out there as soon as might be convenient. ' I have much to tell you,' he said, ' much to tell indeed.' His disembodied voice had a more theatrical quality than I had ever noticed before.

I immediately drove out to the house. It seemed to me that the butler contemned me for answering so speedily to Buzbee's summons. While he went to enquire just where Mr Buzbee was about the place, I contemned him in turn for his lack of insight into the complex realities of the situation. Also for the likelihood, given his parasitic and anachronistic status in the social system, of his complacent indifference to the basic issues involved in relation to our community and its future.

He returned to say that Mrs Fitzpayne was resting after the journey, but that Mr Buzbee was in the pond garden. I told him I knew my way to it. This pond garden was situated a couple of hundred yards from the back of the house, beyond beds of flowers, a wide lawn, a shrubbery and a steep bank into which had been built a broad approach of six or seven stone steps with massive balustrades. The garden itself was in fact a lawn having in the middle of it a large circular pool with statuary, and fountains which may possibly have been modelled on those in Trafalgar Square. Mrs Fitzpayne, with whom I had occasionally walked there, was notably uninterested in the date or style of any of the embellishments of her house. It was, I had always thought, a bull-point in relation to my own plans. This disinterest, I believed, would cause her to be the more easily dislodged. Nor, I had observed, did she take the slightest notice of the nondescript statuary placed at irregular intervals around the edge of this sunken garden. Some pieces, representing single figures in togas, might be presumed to represent ancestors of the original owners of the house. Others consisted of figures of classical mythology.

As I moved through the narrow belt of the shrubbery I saw the figure of a man, whom I took to be Buzbee, seated with his back to me on the level marble surface at the top of the balustrade. Only his back and shoulders were visible, his head being sunk as though in thought. I was about to hail him when, no doubt catching the sound of my steps, he straightened himself, raised his head and sat motionless, perhaps listening. The man was entirely bald.

I stepped forward a little more slowly, preparing myself to meet this stranger who might represent some new factor in the situation. As I did so the man got up from his seat, turned, and Buzbee's familiar face confronted me. He came towards me, both hands extended in greeting. From one of them, at the end of a piece of elastic, dangled a silvery wig.

I cannot say I was speechless. On the contrary I could hear myself babbling more or less incoherent greetings as we advanced to within hand-shaking distance. It was by no means like meeting a man hatless whom you have previously only seen wearing a hat. Buzbee without his wig, though recognizably Buzbee, gave the effect of being a new, more or less profoundly different personality. Different in precisely what way I could not immediately clarify to myself. But what struck me most forcibly was simply this: I should certainly have expected the general impact, so to speak, of an habitual wig-wearer to be diminished by the removal of his wig. Why, one would have thought, if it were otherwise, should he wear it in the first place? Buzbee on the contrary seemed in some indefinable way to be enhanced. This effect may have had something to do with the fact that whereas, bewigged, he had roughly the appearance one might expect of any good-looking Englishman of what is sometimes called the 'clubman' type, his bald skull with its massive bone-structure seemed built on more exotic and grander lines. At least in my first confusion of thought, I was reminded of a picture I had seen of the head of some Mongol or Turkoman conqueror.

After a couple of minutes' chit-chat – weather in London and coastwise, bad state of the railways, mutual health, etc – he put an arm across my shoulders and said, 'Come and walk with me. The marble I have been sitting on is deliciously warm from the sun, but a little hard.' At the same time his other hand was playing with the wig like a hairy yo-yo. I could not take my eyes off it. He looked from me to it and laughed.

'You never detected it? The maker will be flattered. A fine bit of work. All the same, what a relief it sometimes is to take it off. You may think me irrational, but to do so gives me a curious sense of – how shall I put it? – security. Yes, I think security is the word.'

Since I found his last remark too obscure for comment, I said nothing as we descended the steps. But obscure as it was the statement was still alarming: what would happen to this sense of security as and when he learned of Edwina's catastrophic behaviour? It would surely have been better that he should have felt rather less secure at that moment. In his present mood, whatever its cause, the shock must certainly be extreme. A half-hour earlier I had decided that my best tactical plan would be to approach the subject myself. In that way, it had seemed to me, I might hope at the very outset to suggest to him that this sad business, and in particular the part played in it by Pete, should not be permitted to influence his actions so far as my project was concerned. Now I changed my mind and decided to say nothing.

Buzbee said, 'Before we talk any sort of business I would like to have a serious chat with you about little Edwina.'

I must have made some lugubrious noise for he said, 'What?' and I said 'Nothing,' and he continued.

' I have never mentioned it to you because, friends though we are, I hesitated to intrude my private concerns upon you. However, things are going on well enough now to enable me to do so without seeming to involve you in anything too bothersome.'

This dismaying remark produced in me a nervous tension so extreme that one of my feet abruptly stiffened, as in cramp, and I stumbled slightly against him. 'Bit of rough going here,' he said, although the ground was as smooth and even as a tennis lawn, and it was obvious that he must suppose me unsteady from drink.

' The fact is,' he went on, ' I have for a long time wondered whether my attitude to my dear Edwina was not a selfish one. There was a time when I tended – perhaps by wishful thinking

– to minimize the importance of the difference, the really enormous difference, in our ages. I have come to realize that it is as important at least in our case as it is conventionally supposed to be. I am not referring to the strictly sexual aspect of the relationship because, well,' he cleared his throat, 'well, because so far as that's concerned I,' he turned a somewhat lewd smile on me, 'I believe there was, shall we say, no cause for complaint. You follow me?'

'Quite.'

'But as regards common interests the gap is wide, perhaps impossibly wide. And then there is the future to be considered. I mean Edwina's future after I am gone as go, of course, we all must. Naturally I have always been ready, though certainly not eager, to perform the act of what is called "releasing" her at any time. But release her to what? Set her on what path? For you must bear in mind that because of her life with me she has not built up the sort of friends and connections which she probably would have had she been teamed with a man nearer to her own age. What it amounted to was that, if my wish for her welfare was to be more than a pious hope, the thing to do, not to put too fine a point on it, was to find a man. Find a younger man. You follow my reasoning?'

'Quite,' I said again.

'And that,' said Buzbee, patting my sleeve with one hand and twirling the wig gaily with the other, 'is where I owe you, my friend, a debt of gratitude. I mean, of course, for having such a brother-in-law as young Nordahl and introducing us to him. Almost, I think, from that first moment I set eyes on him that day beside your pool, I said to myself, "That's the lad for little Edwina." A man headed for the top of his profession, and such muscles. From then on I did all I could to promote the romance, encouraging her to go out with him etcetera. It was so absolutely, if you follow me, *suitable* – like *that*.'

He had stopped suddenly opposite a piece of statuary representing in conventional manner a nymph and a young God of sorts, standing entwined in an embrace.

'Like *that*,' repeated Buzbee heartily, and gave the nymph an enthusiastic smack on her bare behind. 'Let them go to it I said to myself,' he said, fetching her another smack. 'That's the way Nature meant it to be. Carry on young fellow,' he added, addressing the nondescript young God. And to me, 'You see my point. Youth to youth, that's what the doctor ordered.'

'And you think . . .?' I said.

'My spies tell me, just a couple of hours ago on my return, that all goes excellently well. That butler of Norah's isn't such a stuffed owl as he looks. For a little consideration, a little of the good old crinkle, he keeps his eyes and ears open around the place. And the good word is that the whole time I've been away that pair of youngsters have been rolling in the hay up there in the backwoods; place called the Valley Inn, and jolly good luck to them.'

Though it was far from being news to me, I had, in the circumstances, no difficulty at all in registering surprise.

We had now left the nymph and her God-lover, and Mr Buzbee paused in front of a single figure which, except that it wore only a toga, might have been a full-length portrait in marble of Gladstone in late middle-age.

'That's nearer my age group,' said Buzbee, 'than that young feller-me-lad back there. Looks distinguished, doesn't he? Probably one of those stern old Roman judges or senators or whatever that you read about in school. Full of years and wisdom.' He continued contemplating the statue for some seconds in what seemed to me thoughtful and slightly melancholy appraisal. Resuming our walk he said, 'Have you talked much with that butler?'

I said I had hardly exchanged twenty words with the man in my life.

Buzbee looked at me sideways and looked away again.

'I thought perhaps,' he said, 'that while we were away . . . I mean you might have sought information.'

'Certainly not,' I said with some show of indignation, while privately thinking that in the general interests of Security and

Intelligence, so important in any campaign, I would have done well to have cultivated the butler.

'No harm in it,' continued Buzbee, as though I had not denied his suggestion, 'I don't hold it against you at all. Most natural thing to do. Natural for him too. I mean look at it this way. Say I'm working with you on this project of yours. Maybe I want to know a bit more about you. Maybe I think the butler has a little bit of info. A spot of cash changes hands. Mutually profitable transaction. That's business.'

I assured him that nothing of the kind had taken place and again, recalling Edwina's disclosures of Buzbee's past, regretted that it had never occurred to me to nobble, as the saying goes, the butler.

'So,' said Buzbee. 'No offence. I just wondered.'

He stopped walking to contemplate the recumbent figure with toga, of someone who might have been Gladstone in old age. Either the original sculptor or rain and frost had given his face a harassed and ravaged expression as though, I thought, he had just heard of yet another defeat for Home Rule.

Buzbee's air of melancholy deepened. 'Sad, isn't it,' he said, 'to look upon?' After gazing for a moment on the eroded face, he suddenly threw his head back, spread his arms a little, and in a loud voice intoned,

'Tell thou the world, when my bones lie whitening
Amid the last homes of youth and eld,
That once there was one whose veins ran lightening
No eye beheld.'

He remained briefly with his head back, his eyes on the sky, like a singer waiting for his last notes to die away in the auditorium. Then, giving himself a little shake as though to get himself awake after sleep, he said, almost angrily, 'Let's get on. I don't care for that old fellow's looks. It's not healthy to stand eye to eye with him.'

He took me by the arm and actually pulled me away, as if he had found me standing on some dangerous ground.

Twenty-one

Far off in the still air I heard the noise made by the opening of the french windows of the drawing-room. I wondered whether Buzbee had heard it too, and instinctively looked at the wig which he continued to twirl. For it occurred to me as possibly disastrous for the furtherance of my plans that he, in his still unexplained 'security', should permit himself to be caught by Mrs Fitzpayne with his hair literally down. It was not, unfortunately, one of those occasions on which one can say 'It's none of my business'. Every aspect of the Buzbee-Fitzpayne relationship was very much my business.

Since I noted that Buzbee, following his encounter with the statue of the stricken elder, seemed to have fallen into a reverie, I spoke loudly and sharply. 'I think,' I said, 'our hostess has come out to look for us.'

Buzbee's face immediately brightened and became alert. 'You think so?' he said, and starting to stride in the direction of the steps uttered a loud Hulloo! And as he ascended the steps with me behind him, he shouted again, 'Hullo, darling! We're here. Pond garden.' At the top of the steps he stood still and, to my extreme confusion, actually waved the wig above his head like a flag indicating the position of a shipwrecked mariner on a raft. 'Coming! Coming!' called Mrs Fitzpayne's voice, powerful and melodious as the horn of an expensive car. We encountered her as her springy Zulu stride brought her swiftly across the big lawn. To me she waved in a gay manner with a warm 'Hullo, there!' On Buzbee she turned a smile so confidently radiant that one thought of a child seeing Santa Claus. They came together in a brief half-hug, then linked arms and we began pacing towards the house.

'Home again, home again,' she said. 'Great to be back, though London was fine too. All well on your bit of the hacienda?' she asked me, leaning forward to peer round Buzbee's chest with an air of eager interest.

I said everything was fine, and, in view of the situation now disclosed, meant it.

'Then everything's fine all round, simply fine,' she said. 'And will be finer still when we get a drink.' And when we did get our drinks she, sitting snuggled against Buzbee on the sofa, raised her glass and said joyously, 'Who's like us?' and with that actually patted the massive bone structure of Buzbee's bald head. The scene, delightful in its implications for the success of my own undertaking, caused me to reflect on the probable truth of remarks made by Edwina in the bar of the Valley Inn by way of explaining the form of the 'love' she had once had for Buzbee. In her case, she had suggested, the sense of security he gave her had become somehow indistinguishable from love in the conventional, including the sexual, sense of the word. On Norah Fitzpayne, I judged, the feeling that she had entranced the most dangerous bloodhound, so to speak, in the kennels of the tax collectors' Gestapo, might, in view of her basic preoccupations, naturally be expected to have a similar effect. Nor did I fail to recall Buzbee's recent rather coarsely boastful hint in reference to what he had called 'the sexual aspect' of his relationship with Edwina, of which she had 'no cause for complaint'.

This latter thought was underlined when, after two or three drinks, Norah Fitzpayne said to Buzbee that she wanted his opinion of some letters that had come to the house while they were away in London. They were, she said, upstairs in her 'work room', forgetting that I knew perfectly well that she had no 'work room' either upstairs or anywhere else in the house. She pulled him to his feet and said to me, 'You'll stay for dinner, won't you, and sort of celebrate everything. Ring up Irma and see if she'll come. Make her come. I'll send the car down for her. Meantime, take a drink, take a nap, take what you like just while we're busy with the business.'

A maid came in, took away the glasses the other two had used, wiped a table on which Mrs Fitzpayne in her exuberance had spilled some liquor. Later the butler came in, apparently on a routine tour of inspection. He opened the closed french windows and closed them again, and moved a pile of illustrated papers from one table top to another. He still looked like a stuffed owl, but was now known by me not to be one. My reaction from my earlier, mistaken estimate was such that I now inclined to the belief that any owl-like quality he might have must be that of sagacity. By unknown means he had become cognizant with all the goings-on at the Valley Inn. It had been apparent from Buzbee's remarks that he knew, or at least that Buzbee supposed him to know, something about Buzbee himself which Buzbee imagined that anyone associated with him in a project might wish to know too. It seemed to me at that moment possible that this man knew everything, or at least was an inexhaustible mine of valuable information into which it would be frivolous negligence not to sink a shaft.

'Mr Buzbee,' I said, 'seems in remarkably good form.'

'Quite so, sir,' said the butler, laying out the illustrated papers in neat order. 'Looks, if I may say so, sir, like a man that's just going to pull off a nice little business coup.'

'I've never,' I said, 'been entirely clear as to just what line of business Mr Buzbee is in.'

'Real estate business, as I understand it. Houses, land, that sort of thing.'

To me this was an encouraging statement. It indicated that Buzbee must have been talking to Mrs Fitzpane, even in the butler's presence, about my plans for the disposition of her house.

I said, 'It would be a great thing for the people of the town if some of his plans came off.'

'It would indeed, sir.'

More than ever impressed with the extent of his information and understanding, I found myself regarding him with the awe some people feel at the thought of a computer. Perhaps if one only fed him the right questions he would come up with all the answers. He might even, I thought rather wildly, know what were the prospects of my hotel breaking even before the end of the summer season.

I said, 'And you think his local business is nearly completed?'

He gave a leer which, to my eye, transformed his face from owl to vulture. 'That'd be telling, wouldn't it, sir?' he said, as he walked towards the door. I remembered Buzbee's reference to the 'good old crinkle' in return for which this butler's services might be available. I could not risk the humiliation which would be involved in proffering such crinkle as I could spare and having it rejected as inadequate. As he closed the door I felt – my nerves being greatly strained by the surprises of the afternoon – that this closing of the door upon knowledge which could be of benefit to the community unless crinkle could change hands was indeed symbolic of the state of affairs in which we lived.

In reply to my telephone call, Irma refused the dinner invitation on the ground that her presence could tend, by giving the thing the air of an ordinary social gathering, to reduce the possibilities of 'getting down to the brass nails' of my project. This seemed to make sense. But by the time the three of us had sat down to dinner it was evident that serious business was unlikely to be at all high on the agenda, if indeed it was going to figure there at all. The atmosphere was such that to introduce any subject of the kind would have seemed like intruding upon a honeymoon couple with questions about mortgages or hire purchase.

Buzbee propounded the view that a few glasses of burgundy formed the ideal buffer between the whisky we had recently been drinking and the champagne we were about to drink, and in this view we concurred. The elated mood of my companions, and my own sense that all this meant that things were conspiring together for good, combined to overcome my normal dislike of champagne. Or possibly this was finer champagne than I had ever drunk before. After a couple of glasses of it I felt in all honesty impelled to pronounce it publicly the finest I had ever drunk. Norah beamed at me.

'After all,' she said, 'it's Independence Day in the United States. So that's fine. Everything's turning out fine. Coming up roses like the man said. You know, of course,' she added, raising her glass in a general toast, it seemed, to whomsoever it might concern, 'that little Edwina's gone sporting off with that godlike brother-in-law of yours? Norway Pete?'

I said Buzbee had just told me of this development.

'Well now,' she said, 'isn't that just simply great? Everybody's doing great.'

At this point Buzbee began to hum, was even, it appeared, singing almost under his breath.

'Sing up,' said Norah Fitzpayne. 'What's the song? Let's all hear it.'

'Unsuitable for a lady's ears,' said Buzbee. 'A soldier's song from that first Great World War. It's indecent. Ribald. Wouldn't dream of singing it here.'

'Balls,' said Norah Fitzpayne. 'Sing up.'

'It's sort of a parody,' said Buzbee, 'of another song that was popular at that time among the populace. Sister Suzy's Sewing Socks for Soldiers. That was the nice version.'

'Before my time,' said Norah sharply. 'Cut the cackle and sing the one you tried to keep all to yourself.'

Buzbee took a gulp of champagne, threw himself back in his chair, puffed out his chest and let go in a loud rough baritone, singing,

'Sister Suzy's selling syph to soldiers
While mother hawks her mutton down the Strand.
At the Elephant and Castle

Father's hiring out his arstle
So the family is doing
Absobloodymuckinfuckinlutely
Grand.'

'Encore,' cried our hostess.

'Not again,' said Mr Buzbee. 'That little ditty always moves me strangely. I think back on the dark days of 1918. Myself just a wide-eyed kid then, a rough boy in Glasgow's notorious slums, understanding perhaps but little, yet feeling, here in my child's heart, the tragedy of it all as our lads went marching past into the holocaust singing that song.'

'Cheer up,' said Norah Fitzpayne. 'It's all over.'

Seeking in turn to give the conversation a lighter tone I said that at least the song was a tribute to the infinite resourcefulness of the typical British family in meeting the most trying conditions, and their simple pride in their achievement.

I was just concluding these remarks when the butler entered and, bending over towards Mrs Fitzpayne, said with an almost conspiratorial air of discretion,

'You are wanted on the telephone, Madam.'

'Who is it?'

'Long distance Madam.'

'But who?'

'He preferred not to give his name, but I have no doubt it was Mr Groom. His voice is familiar.'

'Too damn familiar,' said Buzbee.

'Shall I tell him you are coming on the line, Madam?'

At this something happened which astounded me. Mrs Fitzpayne looked at Buzbee with a query in her look. Buzbee gently shook his head. She said to the butler, 'No. Tell him I'm tired.'

'Yes, Madam,' said the butler, who seemed as much taken aback as I was. 'Shall I ask him to call again in the morning?'

Buzbee said to Norah, 'Better you call him some time.'

She said to the butler, 'No. Tell him I'll call him some time; tomorrow or day after.'

167

I sat marvelling at the power of Buzbee over this woman and rejoicing in it. Thus exalted, I felt, as we left the dining-room, a powerful impulse to move about the vast square footage of this house and picture it as it would be. I particularly wanted to see again the place which Norah called the Crystal Palace. And in fact it may be that this construction, designed originally as a giant conservatory, may really have been a modish mid-nineteenth-century imitation of the original Crystal Palace. It was approached through a great oblong place, once the ballroom. It opened directly into the Crystal Palace with the idea, I suppose, that exhausted dancers could rest or conceal themselves among the palms and other flora which once had filled it. The 'palace' itself extended into the grounds, surrounded by trees and joined to the house only at one end.

Like the ballroom itself, it was two storeys in height, and tonight, with only the moon to light it, we could only just make out the curve of the great roof of glass and iron forty feet or so above our heads. In many places the moonlight itself was interrupted by thick mats of bird-droppings. I made up my mind that this would be an ideal recreation room for the children in winter or on cold or wet days at other times of the year. My enthusiasm was such that I barely restrained myself from uttering what was in my mind. Realizing that to do so could be tactless, premature, I rationed myself to a cry of 'Splendid! Magnificent!' as I saw in my mind's eye the future happiness of those poor children.

'Splendid it may be,' said Norah, 'but just now it smells to me of rats or bats and looks like one of the hangars the airline forgot. Let's get back to civilization.'

We trekked back through that long ballroom which I now mentally divided into two spacious, airy and, when the sun would shine, sunlit places of learning for all those eager, weary, frustrated children.

'People,' I said, talking off the top of my head to Norah Fitzpayne, 'say they are the treasure of the future. The promise of our country's well-being in years to come. I say they are the treasures of today and Goddamn the bloody future.'

'Whoever they are you're talking about,' she said, 'you're Goddamn right. The hell with the bloody future. What we need now is a little brandy and a lot more champagne.'

We had that, and I said I must be going. They begged me to stay the night. I refused. They begged me not to attempt to drive the car. I was, they said, in no condition to do so. I agreed. They said the butler would drive me. I refused. I had determined to walk home in the moonlight, through the young woods and then by the beach road.

'He *does* want,' sang Buzbee, 'to be beside the seaside, he *does* want to be beside the sea.' He saw me to the door and at the last moment carefully pushed into the baggy pocket of my jacket a bottle of the brandy we had been drinking. 'For the road,' he said. 'Keep right on to the end of the road.'

I was already down the steps and on to the gravel when I heard his voice raised again. Standing at the top of the steps, between the moonlit central pillars of the portico, he had extended his arms and was reciting in a voice which could have been heard all the way down the far slope to the spot where Colonel Fitzpayne's car had long ago had its notable accident,

'Roll on,' Buzbee recited, 'my song, and to after ages
Tell how, disdaining all earth can give,
He would have taught men from wisdom's pages,
The way to live.'

I went on down through the woods, tripping here and there and even reeling but not, to my satisfaction, absolutely falling. Long after I must, in fact, have been out of earshot I seemed to hear Buzbee's voice booming on like a rhythmic buzzing in the ears, and this sensation, combined presently with the scintillations of the moonlight on the waves of the sea, caused me to think it prudent to seat myself for a few minutes on the grass verge of the coast road with the idea of taking a steadying pull at the bottle of brandy. To my dismay (for having decided to have a drink of brandy, a drink of brandy had become an essential), I realized that Buzbee, acting hastily on a generous

F*   169 impulse, had forgotten to provide me with a corkscrew. There are, I believe, people who by a quick, circular frictional movement of the hand of the palm against the bottom of a bottle of spirits, can cause the cork to fly out. I had attempted this trick too often in past emergencies without success to risk a similar rebuff now. And I shrank from the idea of knocking off the top of the bottle with a stone.

Wondering, somewhat hopelessly, whether somewhere along the route there might be a dwelling where a corkscrew could be borrowed, I recalled with a chill of disgust that the first house on this road was 'Harrogate's Harem'. That, I was just saying to myself, is a non-starter when, at a bend in the road I saw a little ahead of me what seemed to me in my excited condition a blaze or galaxy of lights, many of them seemingly coloured. And as I advanced I could hear voices raised in song. The words I could not hear, but the tune was that of John Brown's Body. In my relief at the sound of such good cheer, I shouted. A man and a woman appeared to be doing some kind of dance under the lights decorating the front of the little house.

I shouted again, the singing stopped. The two figures drew apart. The man, now seen to be Harrogate himself, took a step along the brief flagstone path leading from the open front door to the road. 'Who goes there?' he shouted, as loudly as I had shouted, although we were now within a few yards of one another. Then, as I came more clearly into his field of vision, he gave a series of loud ejaculations. 'You? You? You?' I sensed that each 'you' expressed a different emotion – astonishment, annoyance, finally doubt as to the evidence of his eyes.

My obsessive thought about him then and there was quite simply that what I had here was a man who was visibly drunk and who, it seemed to follow, was likely to have a corkscrew somewhere within reach. 'It's me, Harry old boy!' I could hear myself shouting. 'Have a drink!' and I waved the brandy bottle at him. At this Eileen, the secretary girl-friend, rushed forward, and started to grab at my arm shrieking, 'Don't you dare touch him.' I eluded her and lowered the bottle. At that she straddled her legs, put her arms akimbo and with venom uttered the words 'Limey go home.'

While I stood confused by this strange form of attack, she abruptly threw out one arm in the direction of the house and in a strained voice, half swallowed by emotion, declaimed, 'Shoot if you will this old grey head, but spare my country's flag.'

Following the direction of her gesture, I saw that not only was the front of the house decorated with a number of what are called 'fairy lights' but that from a first-floor window projected a short flagstaff from which hung the Stars and Stripes. I then hazily recalled that I had heard somewhere that Eileen's father had been an American and that she had, as a child, been at school in the United States. The situation became clearer when she again turned to me and shouted, 'Don't you know what day it is, you low Limey, you? Fourth of July for ever! Give me liberty or give me death!'

Harrogate who had at first started back at the sight of the brandished brandy bottle now stepped between us in conciliatory fashion. 'Limey he may be,' he said. 'So'm I, comes to that. One hundred per cent. And look what he's done, oh girl, oh girl! Brought us a great bottle of booze to celebrate Independence Day. Come inside, old pal,' he said to me, 'the night is yet young. Let joy be unrefined.'

'Corkscrew?' I said.

'Dozens of them,' said Harrogate leading the way to the front door of the cottage which opened directly into the living-room. On the central table empty wine bottles together with partially full bottles of vodka and whisky formed a platoon in front of a huge iced cake topped with two tiny flags – the Union Jack and the Stars and Stripes. Snatching up a corkscrew and jabbing it into the cork of my bottle Harrogate said, 'Talk about corkscrews. This fellow thinks I'm crooked as a corkscrew. Don't you Jim, old man, old man? Come off it. Of course you do. Crooked as a bloody corkscrew.' Laughing loudly, he filled three glasses with brandy, and Eileen, now laughing too, and giving me friendly pats on the cheek, raised her glass and shouted, 'My country may she ever be right, but right or wrong my country!'

'That's something we can all drink to,' said Harrogate, gulping it down. Re-filling the glasses he said, 'Come, let us appreciate the moonlight and the balmy night air, so soothing to the nerves of the city-dweller, which makes of this section of our coast a veritable Mecca at journey's end.'

'Glory, glory,' chanted Eileen as we moved again into the open.

Harrogate stood gazing out across the shining sea and his mood suddenly became sombre.

'We,' he said presently, 'stand here gazing upon that peaceful scene, all unwitting that beyond that last, lost horizon lurk such perils as our sturdy West Country forefathers never dreamed of.'

He held his glass in his left hand and raised the other above his head in the gesture of an orator admonishing multitudes.

'Today, aye this very night, giant tankers sail the seas. Ships, my friends, at the size of which your imagination may well boggle. They bring us the life blood of this nation of ours, and who are we to say them Nay? Yet I say to you my friends, beware! Once before one of those great tankers crashed against these shores, wreaking devastation and heavy financial loss, only kept within bounds by those of us who stood ready and willing to fight the oil upon the beaches. We never surrendered.

'What happened before,' he said, turning to left and right and then front again, 'may happen again. I see in my mind's eye one of those oil-laden giants, now a blazing pyre, headed full speed ahead for our shore. There is none aboard to stop her. Her engine-room is an inferno. Her captain and crew have leapt in terror from her deck only to perish in the flaming waters. On and on she roars, a million-gallon torch of death and destruction. She strikes – and within minutes sheet upon sheet of inexorable flame sweeps through our streets and homes, reducing our town in a single hour to the ashes of Sodom and Gomorrah.'

He ceased gesturing, nodded heavily two or three times, took a swig from his glass and turned from one to the other of us with a broad smile.

'And what's to do about it?' he asked. 'Sweet bugger all, that's what.'

An hour later, with the brandy low in the bottle and after a rather incoherent rendering by Eileen of the Battle Hymn of the Republic, to which Harrogate simultaneously sang some of the words of John Brown's Body, he offered to drive me to my hotel. Doubting whether I could get there on my feet I accepted this dangerous offer.

'Car's up the side-lane here,' said Harrogate. 'Reasons of what they call Security, get me? Tattling tongues everywhere.'

Considering the bright chains of the fairy lights, not to mention the noise we had made, I thought confusedly that attention might have been drawn to the house, car or no car. I mentioned this to Harrogate. He replied in a tone of dignified rebuke, 'Not the same thing at all. Fourth of July. Independence Day. Altogether different pair of shoes.'

Although he drove with fair steadiness, at the entrance to the town a patrolling constable halted us. His approach seemed to me menacing. But on seeing who was at the wheel he said, 'Ah, it's you, Mr Harrogate. You all right, Sir?'

'All right, officer?' said Harrogate. 'Of course I'm all right. My friend here's all right too. And you're all right, old cock.' He re-started with a jerk and on leaving me at my hotel gave me a grave salute and departed.

Twenty-two

Waking towards midday I rapidly passed the events of the previous afternoon and evening in review before my mind, seeking to decide what adjustments, if any, of general attitude or particular tactics might be considered necessary in the light of them. I had reached the broad, though admittedly vague conclusion that, while some fresh sidelights on the character of various individuals had been obtained, in the main the only notable change consisted in an alteration in the tempo rather than the nature of my operation. For there was no question that Buzbee's masterly control of Norah Fitzpayne had developed faster than I had dared to hope. Moving to, as it were, the periphery of the entire affair, I could not absolve myself from a sense of having acted to some extent indelicately towards Harrogate, so soon to be confronted with a *fait accompli* likely to cause him grievous worry and embarrassment. I had to admit that by accepting the hospitality of himself and Eileen I had been guilty of a breach of taste caused, quite unquestionably, by an uncontrolled lust for liquor.

Remorse at the thought was deepened by realization that there was nothing that I could do to compensate Harrogate for having, in effect, masqueraded as boon companion and pal when in reality I was far otherwise. This thought might have continued to depress me had I not been interrupted by heavy

174

knocking at my bedroom door and the aggrieved voice of Farragut telling me that there was a man below to see me. What sort of man? What was his name?

'A bloody fidgety sort of man since you ask my personal opinion,' said Farragut. 'There was I setting things to rights in my bar and he comes in and asks where you are and I say you're probably where I wish I was after the late night I had last night with a bunch of Yank tourists celebrating their Independence Day or whatever. And this man says could I just let you know he's there and I tell him to keep his hair on and sit down quiet somewhere till I've got my bar to rights and he sits down for a little while and then there he is again, shooting out his wrist with his watch on it, meaning to be ostentatious, and says he's in a hell of a hurry and will I please go and tell you now and I say okay okay and here I am.'

'But what's his name?'

'He told me,' said Farragut, 'but he had me so rattled I forgot it on the way upstairs.'

'Well, you might go and find out and come and tell me. I shall be in the bath.'

In a few minutes Farragut was there again, shouting through the bathroom door. 'Boom,' he seemed to be shouting above the noise of the running taps.

'You say his name's "Boom"?' I shouted back, turning off the taps.

'Look for yourself,' shouted Farragut, sounding more aggrieved than ever. 'Gave me his little bit of card. I'll put it under the door.'

I bent to snatch it up before it could become sodden on the damp tiles.

It was the card of Ashleigh Groom.

Absurd though it may seem, I admit that I only just succeeded in stopping myself from calling after Farragut to tell him there must be some mistake. Then I realized that impulse resulted simply from the fact that for so long Ashleigh Groom had been in my consciousness as nothing but a repeatedly intrusive, thwarting voice on the telephone or else a disembodied opinion, usually negative to my plans, reported to me by Mrs Fitzpayne. Now it was as though the Invisible Man, hostile at that, had taken on flesh and was tapping his toes impatiently down there in the lounge. Shaved and bathed, I tiptoed down the stairs and into my office where I poured myself a stiff drink in preparation for confronting this phenomenon.

My first notion on entering the lounge was that it was empty; that the Invisible Man had resumed invisibility. Then there was a movement in the corner of the sofa under the window. Narrow, wispy lengths of grey cloth seemed to stand on end and were seen to have a thin pink face on top of them, itself topped by wisps of yellow hair. The overall impression as this figure advanced, carrying a hat in his left hand and a slim walking stick hung over his left forearm, was one of fragility. As we introduced ourselves and shook hands his nervous jerkiness was such that the stick somehow jumped off his arm, and as he bent to pick it up his hat fell from his hand.

I led him back to the sofa and asked him what he would have to drink. He said, 'No, no, no, no, no, nothing thank you,' with the nearly stuttering anxiety of someone who might suspect himself about to be drugged or poisoned. 'But you have one,' he said, 'you have one, you have one.' I said I would, and rang for Farragut. I was going to add something to the effect that I had had a hard morning. Then it occurred to me that to invent, for the benefit of this Groom, a story in explanation for taking a drink by myself at that hour would induce in me an undesirable state of psychological inferiority with regard to him. I ordered a double whisky.

After Farragut had brought the drink and then gone out of sight, Groom said, 'I daresay you've some idea of what I've come to see you about, some idea?'

I said I had no idea whatever. I had hated him at the other end of a telephone for weeks. I did not feel inclined to be helpful to him now in his state of obvious embarrassment.

He said that he was calling on me because I was a friend of Mrs Fitzpayne and an associate, he understood, of Mr Buzbee. Groom looked quickly round the lounge as though afraid it might be bugged for sound. Then surprisingly he said, 'D'you know, I think I will have a drink after all. A large pink gin.'

In ordering the drink from Farragut I deliberately emphasized that Mr Groom wanted a *large* pink gin thinking to embarrass him further by indicating that it was unusual for the guest to specify the size of his drink.

Sipping it, Groom said, 'The matter is delicate, delicate, delicate.'

I said, 'All right, so it's delicate. But what is it?'

'As you may know,' said Groom, 'I have for a long time been Mrs Fitzpayne's financial adviser. I have, in effect, advised her about financial matters. Quite recently I have noticed a considerable change, a very considerable change in her attitude. She had become, if I may say so, recalcitrant. I would say recalcitrant.'

'She rejects your advice?'

'She appears to accept it but then fails to act upon it. Naturally I became perturbed, for her sake. Very large sums are involved. Very large sums.'

'So I imagine.'

'I naturally took certain steps to find out just what had caused this change. I learned of her association with this man Buzbee. The climax, I may call it a climax, came last night when she refused to speak to me on the telephone.'

I listened with pleased equanimity.

He said, 'And then I learned that she and this Buzbee are about to marry. Marry.'

I said '*Marry?*' and he said, 'Yes, marry. Also, under the influence of this man, she is proposing to dispose of her house. An extraordinarily rash step. I have told her so over and over again.'

It was so evident that his information had come from that nearly omniscient butler that it seemed hardly worth while to enquire what his sources were.

I asked him why exactly he had come to me? What did he suppose I could do in the given situation? Naturally my real purpose was to find out what, if anything, he knew about my project; whether he had, for example, any inkling that it was I who was responsible for the introduction of Buzbee to Norah Fitzpayne, and that the 'disposal' of the house under the 'influence' of Buzbee was in reality the culmination of my plan for the community which Buzbee was so effectively furthering.

He said that since I was acquainted with both the parties concerned, he hoped I might throw some more direct and accurate light upon the situation: was, for instance, this report of an impending marriage well-founded? I said that I had heard nothing of it, but would not, quite frankly, be much surprised if it proved true.

Well then, in that case, Groom said, what was known of the man Buzbee? What precisely was his position in the S S T D ? He referred to the S S T D with such easy familiarity that for a moment I almost forgot that the organization did not exist; was a product of Buzbee's powerful and strategically effective invention. While pretending to reflect upon what I knew of Buzbee's official position in the hierarchy of that imaginary body, I recalled that Groom had himself heard of it for the first time from Norah Fitzpayne, an occasion upon which, in defence of his own status as an expert and a possessor of all relevant inside knowledge of such matters, he had pretended that the name, or at least the initials, were well known to him.

'Naturally,' I said, 'his work being of a confidential nature he has never discussed it at any length with me. However I have gathered . . .'

Groom broke in excitedly to say, 'Yes, yes, you have gathered, gathered, gathered?'

I realized that he not only believed in the existence of the S S T D, but could imagine circumstances under which he, no less than Mrs Fitzpayne, might be terribly menaced by it.

'I have gathered that he functions in one of its highest – how shall I say? – echelons.'

The phrase had the intended effect upon Groom. He gasped, and in a harassed, not to say terrified manner, repeated several times 'highest echelons'.

He swallowed the rest of his drink and seemed to be talking

to the ceiling, saying that he was between the devil and the deep sea. Then turning to me he said:

'After she wouldn't speak to me on the telephone last night and in view of something I subsequently heard, I felt there was nothing for it but to come down here by the very first train in the morning.' He turned to me. 'May I use your telephone?'

'In view of what happened last night,' I said, 'might it not be better simply to turn up at the house? You can always say you tried to telephone in advance but the line was engaged or the exchange was out of order or something.'

I was genuinely anxious that he should gain admittance to the Fitzpayne house. There could be no harm in his acquiring and passing on to me any information that might not already be in my possession: about, for example, this supposedly impending marriage. After fussing with his glass, his hat and his stick he said yes, that would be the best plan.

'I hope,' he said, 'I may call on you later. For consultation. For consultation so to speak.'

I told him I would be delighted. As we parted I could not restrain myself from remarking that I hoped he had some extra crinkle ready for the butler.

He said 'Crinkle? Crinkle?' and left the lounge like an agitated wraith.

At lunch I entertained Irma with an account of the happenings on the previous evening and in the early hours of the morning. She said, 'You see, the process of Americanization. It was their Independence Day. So the Fitzpayne household has a beano, Harrogate goes out on the tiles, and Farragut becomes so stoned that this morning he is nearly immobilized.'

'Probably Groom will have found the people up at the house in the same condition.'

'In that case he would not have stayed for lunch there as he presumably has.'

'Unless he had a working lunch in the butler's pantry.'

'Or has fled the coop altogether, unwilling to share with you whatever information he has acquired.'

But this hypothesis proved incorrect. In the early afternoon I heard, from my office, Groom's voice quaveringly enquiring for me. The day being one of brilliant sunshine, I ordered drinks and led him out to the lawn. Again he chattered in banal fashion – remarking, for instance, that roses were a nice sort of flower to have – until Farragut had brought the drinks and retired.

When were were alone he said, 'Things are much as I thought. The marriage will take place at an early date. A very early date.'

'Good,' I said, speaking with enthusiasm, for this seemed to ensure the success of my scheme; to make it, so to speak, official.

'You think so?' Groom said. He added, in a tone of frank and simple melancholy, 'I don't know where it will leave me. Or,' he added, quickly resuming the role of the trusted and vigilant financial adviser, 'where it will ultimately leave Mrs Fitzpayne. Strictly between ourselves, I mean between ourselves, I don't trust that man Buzbee. Since I was unable to see her alone I had no opportunity to speak to her in this sense. I shall try to do so later. I may be able to persuade her to see me alone in London for consultation. Consultation on matters arising.'

Although I considered his chances of successful interference in the course of events minimal, I thought it wise to speak as discouragingly as possible. 'If you don't mind my speaking frankly,' I said, 'if I were you I should accept the situation. Cut your losses, if any. After all, it would seem that Mrs Fitzpayne is quite under Buzbee's spell. And in any case I hardly suppose you want to tangle with the S S T D?'

'No,' Groom said. 'Not that, of course. Still, I might still render some useful service by making a little investigation of Sun Hotels.'

'Sun Hotels? What are they? Where do they come in?'

'I thought you knew all about it. I was talking about it this morning.'

'I don't recall your mentioning them.'

'Perhaps I didn't mention the name. It's the development group that this Buzbee has persuaded Mrs Fitzpayne to sell the house to.'

I reached slowly for my glass and drank. 'How's that again?' I said. For a moment I thought my suddenly taut stomach was going to throw the whole drink up.

'That's the position,' said Groom. 'It would appear that Buzbee has quite recently established a connection with this group which aims to acquire a number of large properties on the south coast for conversion into luxury hotels. He has also, or at least so I deduce from sundry indications let fall, persuaded Mrs Fitzpayne that a sale to them would in some way which is by no means clear to me, regularize her tax position and fully appease the S S T D. I gather the contract is to be signed very shortly. Like the marriage contract,' he added, with a feeble giggle such as might be expected to be produced by this puny wraith.

'You are sure of your facts?' I managed to say.

'Certainly,' said Groom. 'Mr Buzbee was good enough, good enough, to show me certain correspondence between himself, Mrs Fitzpayne and this group. There were even certain figures which I am, of course, not in a position to divulge.' He looked at me and gave a violent nervous twitch. 'I say,' he said, 'are you feeling all right?'

'Quite,' I said, feeling the whisky settle and feeling it safe to pour a little more on top of it. 'I should advise you, however, in the interests of Mrs Fitzpayne to take a good look at the *bona fides* of Sun Hotels.'

'But I thought you were just advising me against doing anything of the sort.'

'In a general way,' I said, 'I was. But I didn't at that time know what sort of people were involved. Sun Hotels, indeed!' I exclaimed, and as I framed the words I formed a clear mental picture of this group whose name and existence had until a minute ago been unknown to me.

'You know something about them?' queried Groom excitedly.

'They are,' I said with vehemence, 'unquestionably a bunch of rapacious crooks. Greed, Sir, greed is their sole motive force. In a different and better society than ours they would long since have been sentenced to long terms of imprisonment for vicious anti-social practices.'

'You know something of them, then?' Groom again asked eagerly.

'More than enough. I know that they are the kind of people who, in the interests of the community, must be foiled at every turn.'

I could see that Groom was both impressed and alarmed by my words and manner.

'Of course you realize,' he said, 'that this, this, this is highly slanderous. It's a slanderous imputation.'

'Slander be damned!' I said. Seeing in him at this black moment a potential ally, however feeble, I leaned forward and patted him on the knee. 'Be a man, Groom,' I said, 'be a man.'

His nervous response was to move his knee. He then rose, leaving his drink half-finished, and said, 'Well, in all the circumstances I think the best thing for me to do is to get back to London as quickly as possible and pursue certain enquiries. Enquiries, if you see what I mean.'

I walked with him to the hotel and through it to the front door. I walked towards my car. 'No need to drive me,' he said, as though positively alarmed by the prospect. 'It's only a short walk to the station.'

'True,' I said, waving to him as I got into the car. 'And it's only a short drive to see Mr Buzbee. Good-bye. Keep in touch.'

At the Fitzpayne house, the butler was actually loitering beneath the portico at the top of the steps. It would appear that having eavesdropped on the conversation during Groom's visit, he had foreseen my arrival as the logical next step. Also it seemed to me that his expression was more contemptuous than ever. He told me that Buzbee was in the pond garden, and there I found him, seated on a marble bench in the attitude of

Rodin's Thinker, with his wig on his head.

As I approached, he raised his head as though it were too heavy for him and spread his arms a little in a gesture which was something between a shrug and a supplication.

'Well?' I said, mastering my voice. 'Well?'

'I take it,' said he, 'you have seen Mr Groom?'

I said that I certainly had.

'Then,' Buzbee said, 'I assume he has explained to you the turn events have taken.'

The suggestion that he had been a passive observer of a 'course of events' over which he had no control maddened me. I leaned forward from the hips and swore, since he had dropped his head again, at the top of his wig.

'I understand,' he said, 'I fully understand. I had intended to tell you all about it last night. But I didn't want to do anything that might spoil Norah's little celebration. I wanted happiness for all.'

'Damn that,' I said, 'explain yourself.'

He patted the bench beside him, inviting me to sit down. I remained standing, with folded arms, although my legs were trembling from nervous shock.

'I know,' said Buzbee, speaking to the grass just beyond the toes of his shoes, 'that in your eyes I have acted otherwise than quite straightforwardly.'

'You can underline that,' I said.

'You will understand,' he went on, 'that from the first moment that you propounded to me your scheme for somehow converting this great house into the property of what you called "the community", I took it for granted that that was the merest eyewash. A smokescreen for your real intentions. A formula used for the sake of Security.'

'And why the devil,' I burst out, 'should you have supposed anything of the kind?'

'But it seemed to me to stand to reason. You can surely appreciate that. Who in God's name, I asked myself, would exert himself as you were doing on behalf of a project from which, if you were speaking truthfully, you could not make a profit of any kind. Unless, of course, you were thinking of later standing for Parliament as Member for this constituency. Were you,' he said, briefly lifting his head and looking up at me, ' thinking of doing that? It would be an explanation.'

' I have no such ambitions,' I said coldly.

' I'm glad of that,' said Buzbee, ' very glad, I should be very sorry to have thwarted you in a political career. But after all, as you say, what future is there in Parliament these days? What real power has an M P? Even with their present salaries many of them can hardly make both ends meet. I have often thought we are living in the twilight of democracy.'

I told him to stuff all that.

' I repeat,' he said, ' that I assumed, very naturally assumed, that your true objective was quite other than the one you had – as I thought for reasons of prudence and discretion – outlined to me. There were, of course, as our acquaintance ripened, times when I wondered whether you might, after all, seriously mean what you said about your project; I felt that, if that were so, you were, if I may say so, on a fool's errand. In terms, I mean, of human nature. On the other hand, on the assumption that you were really interested in some sort of business coup, I could not help feeling – and you must forgive me this – that you were not just the type, not fitted by experience or character, to pursue such a transaction to a successful conclusion.'

' You mean,' I said, ' that you didn't take me for a crook or confidence trickster. Thank you.'

Buzbee held up his hand in a restraining gesture.

' Just a moment,' he said, ' while I complete my story. In what seems to you now but a dark cloud you may yet see a silver lining. Having established as you know a very, very happy relationship with Norah Fitzpayne, my wife-to-be as Groom will have told you, I sought ways and means to disembarrass her of this house, which is as you have often rightly pointed out, a tax liability, but to do so with profit.

' Having approached the Sun Hotel group I found them more than receptive to the idea. They were enthusiastic. They grow more enthusiastic as the days pass. They have already conducted a thorough survey of the place and its prospects as a hotel. The deal is, one may say, in the bag.'

'In other words you have carried out a successful double-cross. Or you think you have.'

'Wait,' said Buzbee. 'I spoke of the silver lining. I am not speaking only of the inestimable benefits to this town, to this community, which will flow from the establishment here of a hotel of the character which the people at Sun Hotels envisage. I would mention something somewhat more concrete. A representative of Sun Hotels will be in town in a few days' time. He will call upon you. You will find that he has been authorized to pay to you a substantial, I may say a very substantial, commission on the deal in return for the services you have undoubtedly rendered in, however indirectly, putting Sun Hotels in touch with me.'

Twenty-three

Striding, almost rushing across shrubbery, big lawn, drawing-room and hall to the front door, I found the butler still seeming to be enjoying the view of woodland and sea from the portico. It appeared to me that he sneered, as at a defeated man. I gave him a look in return. 'Just you wait, my complacent friend' was what it was intended to convey. And as I bustled into my car I quickly reviewed, mentally, the means so readily at my disposal for putting, so to speak, the skids under Buzbee, for pulling the carpet from beneath his feet.

Arrived at the hotel I looked for Irma and found instead Harrogate, pacing the lawn and viewing the bay with much the same air of complacency as that shown by the butler. He greeted me jovially from afar.

'None the worse for wear? Independence Day comes but once a year, thank God! Talk about hair of a dog. I thought this morning I'd have to eat a whole hide to do anything about my hangover. By the way, I've just ordered a drink. Better make it two.'

Farragut was emerging with Harrogate's drink. Harrogate shouted to him to make it two.

'Couldn't do with any lunch,' he continued. 'And then just when I thought I'd have to take a pill and get a bit of healthy sleep, I get the good news.'

'What news would that be?' I asked.

'Good God! Haven't you heard? Well, I suppose you couldn't have. That reporter at our local rag rang me up. Seems the press officer of Sun Hotels – that's a big, go-ahead London development company – rang him up. Gave him all the gen. Big story. Be in the paper at the week-end. Cutting the cackle and putting it in a nutshell, this Sun Hotel outfit's signing up to buy the Fitzpayne house and convert it to one of the poshest hotels on the entire south coast of this green and pleasant land. O-ho, my boy. That'll put their noses out of joint, those Irish crooks I could mention not fifty miles away along the coast who think they can compete with us in tourist attraction. Of course I realize,' he said, with a slight change of tone, 'it isn't just precisely what you've had in mind. But you won't mind me reminding you I always said that shot wasn't on the board. A definite non-starter.'

I recalled with a pang my last night's lack of delicacy in accepting the hospitality and sharing the boon companionship of this man to whose policies I was so strenuously opposed. In recompense I would have liked to maintain him in his present cheerful state. I regretted having to dash his hopes. But there seemed no other possible course open to me.

I said, ' Sit down. I've something serious to tell you. You'd better take a drink,' I told him, ' and prepare yourself for a bit of a shock.'

'Always prepared to take a drink. Where's the shock?'

'The shock comes,' I said, 'when you learn that Mr Norman Buzbee, and mind you I don't forget I'm responsible for introducing him to Mrs Fitzpayne, is, to put it quite simply, a fraud, a confidence trickster. His name isn't even Buzbee. It's Bronterre. Or at least it was at the time he was run out of Glasgow after being denounced by a Judge in an embezzlement case in which several of his associates were jailed. Just to make the picture prettier, he didn't get hold of that young girl Edwina by marriage or any other normal means: he bought her from her drunken father.'

Harrogate took another drink and looked at the sea.

'You *know* this?' he said. 'I mean you have, if I may say so, rather a sensational sort of mind.'

'I have the facts from Edwina herself.'

Harrogate did a small shrug. 'Ah, well,' he said, 'you know what young girls are like. I hear she's having a walkout with Pete Nordahl. This story could be just a bit of what d'you call it? Self-justification for leaving Buzbee.'

'Nonsense. She and Pete, too, for that matter know perfectly well that all of it, except the bit about her being bought from her father, can be checked from the Glasgow papers. And the change of name is either properly registered somewhere, or he signs cheques and legal documents in connection, for instance, with this deal about the house, with a false name. Sun Hotels aren't going to like that much.'

'They're unlikely to know about it. Why should they?'

'Their representative is coming down here in a couple of days. He is due to call on me. Knowing that I, for my sins, was the one who brought Buzbee into the business, he's bound to ask me about him.'

'Well, you can say no more than you met him as a guest at your hotel and were impressed by his businesslike qualities, vision or what have you etcetera etcetera.' He ruminated for a moment and then said, 'And anyway, if he's what you say he is, how would he have got a big job with this hush-hush tax outfit he works for; the S S T D? How about that?'

'The answer to that is there isn't any S S T D. He invented it to impress people like Mrs Fitzpayne and, I may say, yourself.'

'Now you're really going round the bend. How could you know a thing like that?'

'I know it because he told it me himself.'

'Told you? You expect me to believe that? Why would he do a crazy thing like that?'

'Just part of his technique,' I said. 'He was even good enough to explain it to me more or less. Typical confidence trick. He wanted to gain my confidence so as to have me get him close to Mrs Fitzpayne. So he starts by trusting me with a secret of his own. He thought that just so long as I thought he was working with me for my project that I've so often talked to you about, I'd keep my mouth shut. And after that it would be too late. Or he could pretend, he may yet, that it was a double bluff: he could say he pretended the S S T D was an invention to cover up the fact that it existed. Who's to check on a *secret* organization?'

'Maybe it was a double bluff at that,' Harrogate said. 'Personally I'm very much inclined to believe that it was. Anyway, getting back down out of the clouds, if I may say so, to reality, what in hell's all this matter to you? Your scheme's well and truly down the drain anyway.'

'You don't seem to realize,' I said vehemently, 'that when Sun Hotels learn about the type of character they're doing business with and start to pull out, we're back to square one.'

Harrogate tossed off what remained of his drink and stood up, standing over me. I was startled to see that he was actually shaking, and shaking, as I could tell from his expression and tone of voice, with pure rage. I would hardly have been surprised if he had spat at me.

'And so,' he said, 'for the sake of your damned twaddling sentimental project as you call it, you're prepared to try to wreck a deal that's going to put this town right on the map, way up in the luxury trade? You'd go tattling to this man from Sun Hotels about a man's past that's all over and ought to be forgiven and forgotten if there's any spark of charity in this world? *You're* the kind that talks about loving his fellow man and then kicks him in the teeth when it suits your book. If you read your Bible which I don't suppose a phoney modern-type like you does, you'd have read where our Lord Jesus Christ says " the greatest of these is charity ".'

'It was St Paul,' I said furiously.

The correction increased Harrogate's rage. 'Shut up while I'm talking,' he shouted. 'You're crazy. Softening of the brain. For two pins I'd get you committed. Wouldn't be too difficult. Everyone knows you're a bloody alcoholic.'

'Have another drink,' I said.

'You think it's funny? And another thing. You're guilty of blatant slander. Never mind whatever happened or didn't happen in Glasgow. You've called the man a professional confidence trickster. And d'you know what I'm going to do right now? I'm going to get into my car and I'm going out there and see Mr Buzbee and suggest he slap a writ on you for it. That'll keep your dirty mouth shut for a bit, anyway.'

He again looked at me as though he might spit and stalked away. I was joined by Irma who had been lurking until he was off the premises. She asked what the devil all that had been about. In the tension of the interview with Harrogate I had nearly forgotten that she as yet knew nothing of Buzbee's abominable treachery. I recounted to her the events of the afternoon. As I concluded, she sat quietly looking at the bank of flowers. Her calm irritated me. 'You don't,' I said, 'seem very much upset.'

'I was thinking what's to be done now. What will have to be done.'

'What's to be done is to expose Buzbee. I propose to blow him clean out of the water.'

'It will take a lot of dynamite.'

'It's I that has the dynamite. He hasn't a leg to stand on.'

'In England the strangest people find legs to stand on. They have a hundred tricks to make the wrong horse win.'

She left me and started to wander among the roses.

Annoyed by her defeatism I determined on immediate action. I visited the offices of the local weekly newspaper. The Editor looked at me, I thought, a little askance and I recalled, too late, that the fellow was a crusading teetotaller.

I started to explain as succinctly as possible the origin of my relations with Buzbee. He disturbed and to some extent unnerved me by several times looking at the clock on the wall, and quite often sniffing in what I considered a deliberately ostentatious way.

I nevertheless plodded on. I have very little knowledge of journalists except what I have learned from books, films and television. But I was confident that when I reached the nub of what they call the 'story', that is to say the disclosure of Buzbee's past, its sensational nature could not fail to grip him. But I had hardly started on this part of my narrative when he interrupted me to say quite coolly 'Look here, Mr Ballantyne, I am sure this is all of great interest to you, but I must tell you right away that it simply is not the kind of material that this newspaper would care to print. Even supposing that the facts are exactly as you have learned them at second hand from an obviously prejudiced party, this man has clearly not committed any provable misdemeanour or felony. To rake up now what some Judge in Glasgow is supposed to have said about him, could, I think, well be held to constitute a malicious libel. I don't say it would, but it is a risk which this newspaper is not prepared to take. And whatever his past, I may say that in my view his action in interesting this hotel group in this development cannot be otherwise than beneficial to the town.'

I suddenly remembered many criticisms I had read of our supposedly free press. The blood rushed to my head. I leaned across his desk and said sharply, 'I believe you are thinking of the advertisements you may get out of this. Call yourself an independent Editor? You're nothing but a pawn and puppet dancing to the dictates of the advertisers.'

As I thrust my face towards him, he actually waved his handkerchief to and fro in front of his nose, half rising as he did so.

'A newspaper,' he said pompously, 'has a duty to consider the interests of its advertisers as it does those of other people. And now Mr Ballantyne I'm afraid we must consider this interview terminated.'

My chagrin was such that I had to hurry across the road to the saloon bar opposite, where I drank enough whisky to loosen the knots which seemed to have formed themselves in my stomach. I felt the need of a talk with some fellow citizen who would see the state of affairs in its proper light and be properly shocked by the way things were being conducted. With this vague notion in mind, I later turned in to the bar of the pub where I had last drunk beer with the cynical but aggrieved father of the children who had played at being Buddhist priests.

He was there, and while I bought us drinks he asked me in his derisive manner how 'all the pie in the sky' I had talked about at our last meeting was coming along. 'Not seen much of it yet, mate,' he said. I began to marshal my thoughts so as to put the position to him in convincing fashion.

'You have to understand,' I began, by way of leading up to the present posture of events, 'that this sort of business isn't all plain sailing. There are a lot of bad characters about. Saboteurs.'

'Only just found that out?' he said, sneering more cynically than ever. 'Listen while I tell you something.' He began a long confusing story of bad things done by some bad characters. I made an effort to bring the conversation back to the subject nearest my heart. But he continued, sometimes to interrupt and sometimes to sneer. In the end he forsook speech and let out such a tirade of farts that I thought it best to leave him.

I had already made an attempt to reach Pete Nordahl and Edwina. But his housekeeper had told me that he had been away for a few days. I assumed they were still on their premature honeymoon at the Valley Inn. But when I telephoned there, some lying manageress, suborned no doubt by Pete in the interests of Security, denied all knowledge of any such couple. I cursed them for their self-centred sex mania, but the following morning did succeed in getting Edwina to the telephone at Pete's town address. I put her, as they say, in the picture. I said I supposed I need hardly spell out the importance of having her confirm to others, in particular to the representative of Sun Hotels, what she had told me of Buzbee.

To my astonishment and disgust she refused. She said she was through with Buzbee, but she did not want to take part, as she put it, in 'hounding' him. I almost screamed with annoyance. It was not, I said, a question of hounding him personally. This was no vendetta. This was an effort to prevent his diverting for private gain what should be a valuable asset to the poor of our community. I demanded to speak to Pete.

He said offensively, when I began to put the matter to him as calmly as I was able, 'Are you sober? Well, if you are then do get it through your head that neither Edwina nor I are interested in your cockeyed schemes. And,' he said, 'there's another thing I want to warn you about. Don't you go and involve my sister Irma too much in this thing. I know and you know what she's like when she once gets the idea there's something that ought to be done. She's capable of anything. You get her over-excited about this thing, she might go and shoot Buzbee or something. Just watch it.'

For whatever motives, and I could think of several, Buzbee, although he had not formally given up his room at the hotel, seemed to have decided to remain holed-up at the Fitzpayne house. There, naturally, he enjoyed every luxury and was able simultaneously to indulge himself sexually with Mrs Fitzpayne while keeping an eye on her in case of any last-minute change of direction on her part. I took advantage of this to search his room in the dim hope of finding something compromising in the way of correspondence or other documents. I found nothing but his clothes, some copies of the coloured brochure about our town which Edwina had mentioned, and a small book or pamphlet on the history and significance of tarot cards. This last had been published some years ago, and was in a much worn condition. Inside the fly-leaf something had been written and then very completely inked out. I made no doubt that it was the name 'Bronterre'.

My only communication with him came a couple of days later via Farragut. Buzbee had left a message stating that Mr Bagehot of Sun Hotels would be arriving in the town that afternoon and would be hoping to see me. Also, would we reserve a room for him ' if there was a room vacant '. This was an implied jeer, since he must know the hotel was now empty. I decided to disregard it. I gave orders for the best room in the house to be made ready for Mr Bagehot. For I sensed that in him I should at last find a reliable ally to assist me in foiling the machinations of Buzbee. I was alert in my office when he arrived from the London train and conducted him personally to his room. I had also forsworn the use of whisky for that day, and during the morning and afternoon touched nothing but vodka on the ground that it is supposed not to be noticeable on the breath.

He was a blond man of thirty or so having, as the old-fashioned books I read when I was a boy used to say of the hero, 'a frank, open countenance'. His clothes, as anyone who was familiar with clothing advertisements in the coloured magazines could see, were correct for the young executive of a go-ahead firm. I took him down to the lounge where, at my request, Irma was already established.

'Well, well,' he said, after I had ordered our drinks, 'this is an auspicious occasion. I think a toast is called for.'

'Look, Mr Bagehot,' I said, 'there is something I have to tell you. And I am afraid you will think it bad news.'

He gave me a look of startled and slightly suspicious enquiry, and lowered the glass he had been raising for the toast.

'I'm sorry to hear that,' he said, his tone one of courteous solicitude, as though I had told him I was the victim of some disease. 'What seems to be the trouble?' He turned to Irma and said with a small smile, 'Part of my job is listening to troubles.'

At last I had an attentive audience for my story. Apart from an occasional question asked to clarify some point, Mr Bagehot listened in absolute silence to all I had to tell him about Buzbee. I did not conceal my own interest in the disposal of the Fitzpayne house, but made no great matter of it either, since I felt it was not the sort of thing that could be expected to interest him. When I had finished I experienced a mixture of elation and relief at having at length managed to convey the facts to a person in a position to take immediate action to put things to rights.

Bagehot remained silent for some time, nodding once or twice at the glass in his hand, as though mentally ticking off one point or another. Then he said,

'Mr Ballantyne, I really am extremely grateful to you for giving me this information. I daresay we might have winkled it out for ourselves had the need arisen. Still, it's good to have it all spelled out for us with so little trouble on our part.'

'I felt sure you would be glad to have the facts,' I said.

'Yes, indeed,' Bagehot said. 'It's always a good thing to have the facts even if one decides, as – I am sure you will agree – one must decide in this case that they really are irrelevant, that's to say not germane to the business in hand.'

'What?'

'Well, you can see as well as I can that, so far as this transaction is concerned, the past or present character of Mr Buzbee hardly enters the picture. He has acted as an intermediary and will be recompensed as such, as will you yourself, I'm happy to say.' He bowed slightly in my direction and continued. 'Although he has, in fact, conducted the negotiations between ourselves and Mrs Fitzpayne, hers will be the signature on all relevant documents. So that at this point I don't think we need any of us worry our heads too much about Mr Buzbee's moral failings.' He did an indulgent type of smile and gently shook his head.

Irma stared at him as though he were transparent and she could see something beyond him. Her expression was so strained that for a moment I wondered whether Pete had not after all made some sense when he warned me against allowing her to become over-excited by the matter at issue. But I was myself too much overcome with astonishment and indignation to give this more than a passing thought.

'But surely the man must be exposed,' I said. 'Surely otherwise we are, I'm not certain of the correct term, we are compounding a felony. Take the business of the s s t d. It was on the strength of that that Buzbee first obtained his hold on Mrs Fitzpayne. It was that which made her act against the advice of Ashleigh Groom. Yet no such organization exists. His representations were fraudulent.'

'As I understand it,' said Bagehot gently, but with an edge to his voice, 'you were aware of the fact that this supposed organization was non-existent *before* you introduced Mr Buzbee to Mrs Fitzpayne. No doubt you were carried away, very understandably of course, by your enthusiasm for your own project. You supposed at that time that Mr Buzbee was acting in the interests of your own very laudable project.'

'That's not the point. I don't care,' I said passionately, 'whether I'm involved or not. In any case the point won't arise. The moment Sun Hotels pulls out, letting him know that you are in possession of all the facts about his past and his fraudulent goings-on, he'll get out of this town in a cloud of dust, like he got out of Glasgow. Or,' and here I saw a truly hopeful aspect of affairs, 'if Mrs Fitzpayne persuades him otherwise, he'll certainly be ready to put himself right by carrying out my scheme as originally promised.'

'Look, Mr Ballantyne. Aren't you being just a little selfish about this? If I hadn't met you I'd almost say just a little spiteful. Don't think I don't sympathize, most sincerely sympathize with you in connection with your plan that's gone awry. We all have these disappointments in life particularly when we're on what I may call the reforming tack. I mean to say think of all those early reformers. Setback after setback. Nearly lynched in the streets, some of them, I believe. Still, it all came out in the wash. But just sticking to the immediate point, I must say I see no reason at all why Sun Hotels should, as you put it, "pull out", still less harass Mr Buzbee with threats or anything of that sort.'

I was speechless.

'And I think I should add, Mr Ballantyne, that in my opinion it really would be most unwise on your part to try to give any sort of publicity, verbal or otherwise, to what are, to put it plainly, exceedingly slanderous statements concerning Mr Buzbee.'

'You mean that to do so might foul up the deal for Sun Hotels?'

'It certainly wouldn't, as you put it, "foul up" the deal. I do admit, however, that it would be from our point of view very distasteful. Particularly in the hotel business, nobody wants to have the smell of some sort of scandal hanging around the start of the operation. You know what people are like. Though, in this case, Sun Hotels is in no possible way im-

plicated in any doings of Mr Buzbee, when it comes to opening the hotel there's always going to be somebody who says
"weren't those people mixed up in some scandal or other?"
and if they're uncertain what place to go to, a thing like that
just tips the scales against us and that could be quite serious.
Particularly at the beginning. It's a cumulative business. It
escalates. One lot of people don't come and then another lot
hears the first lot aren't coming, so they don't come either.'

Irma spoke for the first time since the preliminary introductions. 'Yes,' she said, still seeming to be looking through rather
than at Bagehot, 'I do see how that might be.'

Bagehot bowed courteously in her direction and said he was
glad she appreciated the realities of the situation. 'But,' he
continued, 'though I have mentioned our position, I was really
thinking more of your own. Let me make it perfectly clear first
that whatever action you see fit to take we shall go ahead with
this deal. Should you persist in some attempt to "expose", as
you term it, Mr Buzbee, we should naturally take steps to
show that it was you who knowingly introduced a supposed
confidence trickster into the business. We should also seek the
widest publicity for the view that you, for personal reasons,
were prepared to deprive the town of the benefits of this
development. You will naturally realize that we shall be taking
major advertisement space in the local paper and I suppose we
shall have no difficulty in getting space for our views in the
news and letter columns.'

Without realizing that I was voicing my thoughts I heard
myself saying aloud, 'So there's nothing to be done?'

'In that direction, I'm afraid, nothing,' said Bagehot briskly.
'But since we are, on your part unwillingly I realize, agreed on
that, let me turn to a more positive and I may say more cheerful aspect of the question. I have here the cheque and the
necessary form for signature in respect of the commission
which, as Mr Buzbee pointed out to us, is due to you by way
of commission on services rendered.'

He opened his brief-case and took from it a typewritten
form and a cheque. He handed them to me. I saw that the

cheque was, as Buzbee had said, for a 'substantial' amount. Holding it in both hands with intent to tear it to pieces I said, 'Let me tell you what you can do . . .' but was interrupted by Irma who leaned forward with her hand outstretched and said, 'May I have a look at that?'

Mechanically I handed it to her. To my extreme exasperation she sat silently examining first the cheque and then the accompanying form. I saw Bagehot give a quick look from one to the other of us.

He suddenly looked at his watch and said, 'My goodness! I hadn't noticed the time. Do you mind if I use your telephone for a few minutes? I have to call a man about a thing.' He got up quickly leaving me alone with Irma.

I said harshly, 'What's all this? Tear that bloody thing up and throw the bits in his face.'

'Hush,' Irma said. 'You have just said yourself there's nothing to be done to stop the Sun Hotel deal about that house. To try to do so would be, like they say in English, simply pissing into the wind.'

'We don't have to take money for all this swinery.'

'On the contrary. We must despoil the Egyptians. That house isn't the last pebble on the beach, and you should know it. What about that semi-derelict lot of villas on West Street, the ones with the gardens? Before you ever thought of the Fitzpayne house you thought they could be converted into a school and playground and maybe a couple of flats for the homeless.'

'The owner wasn't willing to sell, far as I remember.'

'Only because he thought he'd an offer from some London firm when all that business of dispersal started. But he hasn't. We could buy the whole thing quite cheap – at least we could try. And then offer it to the town so cheap they wouldn't dare refuse, but make it a condition it was used for our intended purpose. Just like you planned to do with the Fitzpayne place.'

'Are you mad? That cheque's no more than a drop in the bucket of what those buildings would cost, however low the man was ready to sell them at.'

'But,' said Irma, 'it's a beginning. Nothing to be snooted and sneezed at and spurned in vulgar pride. Why should we save Sun Hotels money?'

I hesitated. She said, looking towards the window, 'I think we may even get some more out of them before many moons are passed.'

'That money stinks,' I said.

'You can make it smell better,' said she.

'I was just telling Bagehot what he could do with it.'

'And so now Bagehot will dub you a vainglorious blowhard, whose principles crumble to dust at the touch of lucre. But we should value his opinion no more than we would that of a cockroach. Forward to victory. Sign that form. Sign it.'

The form was brief, simple and straightforward. I read it and, though my hand trembled with nervous indignation, signed it. Bagehot re-appeared a moment later. It was evident to me that he had used the telephone merely as an excuse to leave us together. Probably he had been lurking in the corridor watching us.

I silently handed him the signed form, and with what calm I could achieve placed the cheque in my wallet.

After some civilities Bagehot left us to call at the Fitzpayne house. He returned just as Irma and I were finishing a nightcap drink before going to bed.

'I don't want to intrude,' he said, 'but I just wanted to say that I have been on the telephone to London and now that everything is fixed, it's been arranged that we should have a little ceremony at which the launching of our venture, I mean the conversion of the house into a first-class hotel, will be announced. A couple of our Directors will be coming down for the occasion, of course, and we hope some representatives of newspapers in the major towns of the western and south-western region. And of course a number of leading citizens of this town. I may say that I and my Directors very much hope that despite certain divergencies in our points of view you and Mrs Ballantyne will be among those present. You will of course get a proper invitation card in a day or two.'

I mumbled something or other, and Irma said, ' Thank you, very much. We shall be honoured.' I glared at her, but she appeared unabashed.

Bagehot was about to leave when he said, ' Heavens! I nearly forgot. Mr Buzbee asked me to give you this note.' He handed me an envelope and said good night. Opening the note, I found in it a sheet on which were written in Buzbee's handwriting, four lines from what seemed to be his favourite poem. ' What does he say?' Irma asked. ' He says,' I said, reading aloud:

' And he fell far through that pit abysmal,
   The gulf and grave of Maginn and Burns,
   And pawned his soul for the devil's dismal
   Stock of returns.'

Under this were the words, ' Despite this, try to think of me with charity. Norman Buzbee.'

' Charity!' I said. ' Obviously he has been talking to that crook Harrogate.'

Two days later the card, a big affair with silver lettering, arrived. Before I could say that I refused to go Irma said, ' You must go. It is more than ever essential that you appear to one and all in the capacity of prominent citizen.'

' And you, I suppose,' I said with extreme bitterness, ' will be present as Mrs Truckle and Swallowit.'

She paid me no attention, but continued to examine the card. ' I see,' she said, ' that they are holding the affair in what they call the Glass Pavilion. I suppose that's what everyone else calls the Crystal Palace.'

' In that case,' I said, ' we'd better take Farragut along to help fill the ranks of the prominent citizens. The place is enormous.'

Irma said, ' Norah Fitzpayne showed me round it once, months ago. You know properly heated and so on it would make a wonderful kind of tropical garden. I think it must have been designed as something of the kind originally. There are even pulleys to open up sections of the glass roof so as to keep the ventilation right. It made my mouth water. I shall enjoy seeing it again. Even full or half-full of prominent citizens.'

When I continued hesitant about attending this monstrous ceremony she said, 'Do you wish to advertise yourself as an outcast, a pariah? Do you intend to demonstrate that you are shunned by the higher citizenry? There is nothing that would more rejoice the black hearts of hostile elements.'

Impressed though reluctant I agreed to go. The affair had been scheduled for twelve o'clock noon, with the idea that it would thus have a chance of being reported in the largest circulation daily papers of the nearest cities, which were both evening papers. Irma did, in fact, act on her proposal that Farragut should accompany us. 'He rejoices at a sight of the nobs,' she said. 'It strengthens his battered sense of self-esteem.'

A number of the local 'nobs' were assembled by the time we had arrived and been directed to the Crystal Palace by the butler who wore an air of triumph as if some victory of his own were being celebrated. At the far end of the great glass structure a dais had been erected. On chairs behind a long baize-covered table I noted Norah Fitzpayne, Buzbee, Harrogate and a couple of other town councillors, the abominable Editor with whom I had recently spoken, Mr Bagehot and a couple of strangers who, I assumed, were Directors of Sun Hotels. Thirty or forty 'prominent citizens' and others whom I took to be newspaper reporters, either sat on chairs set out in rows in the body of the place, or strolled about chatting to one another. Two of the Fitzpayne maids moved among them with glasses of sherry on trays.

Encouraged by Irma, Farragut took a glass and drank nervously as though expecting to be warned off. Irma said, 'I've left my basket in the car.'

'What basket? Why a basket?'

'I thought after this is over I might wander about the garden a bit and possibly take some cuttings of plants. Norah Fitzpayne won't mind – she once said I could take anything I fancied for my garden. Obviously the show isn't going to start for ages.'

She turned to Farragut and said, 'Would you please go and fetch the basket from the back of the car and meet me outside, through that side door there. If you wouldn't mind you could stay with me and carry the basket while I take cuttings, if any.'

Refusing sherry, I took advantage of the delay in starting the proceedings to walk quickly back into the main part of the house and get myself a glass of whisky. On my return I found that the personage who seemed to be the principal Sun Hotels Director was already on his feet, addressing the gathering. I took a seat at the end of the second row, waiting for the whisky to take its soothing effect as the river of verbiage flowed placidly over us. It was, naturally, indicated that the Directors of Sun Hotels had for a long time past had a warm spot in their hearts for this town; had cherished it in their dreams; had always hoped that some day, somehow, they would be granted the opportunity, indeed the privilege, of benefiting both themselves and the town by making it the scene of one of their major operations. Now the hoped-for moment had come. After applause, the Director made some remarks in humorous vein which were greeted with small cackles of laughter. He concluded on the deeper note, describing his vision of all that this could mean not just to Sun Hotels, not just to all those lovers of the incomparable south-west coast of Britain and all that it had to offer to the visitor, but also, in terms of prestige and added material prosperity to the town itself.

A scene of enthusiasm was witnessed as he sat down, with Buzbee, Harrogate and the Editor leading the applause. Harrogate, whose high estimate of himself as an orator had seemingly been accepted by his colleagues on the Council, now rose to express on behalf of the town its very very deep and sincere appreciation of the boon conferred on it by Sun Hotels and his confidence that the town, for its part, would more than justify the far-sighted vision and initiative shown by the Directors of Sun Hotels in choosing it as the site for their magnificent stroke of development.

He, too, then reached the point where it was seen fit to introduce a jocular note, Having heard him speak before I would not have been at all surprised to hear him say that a funny thing had happened to him on his way to the ceremony.

But at this point I saw, to my astonishment, that Farragut, who had evidently made his way up the hall on the far side of the rows of chairs, was standing at the edge of the dais. He appeared to be signalling urgently to the nearest member of the platform party. Having attracted the attention of this person, a member of the Town Council, Farragut, so far as I could see from where I sat, handed him an envelope. The Councillor, having glanced at it, passed it to his neighbour and it then went from hand to hand of the people on the dais, to the chief Director, and temporary Chairman. It was evidently to him that it was addressed, for he at once opened it.

As he read it, I observed that he suffered a small nervous twitch, not quite amounting to a convulsion, and then for no reason I could imagine, peered – craning and twisting his neck – upwards at the glass roof above him. Several others on the dais automatically followed his example. I could spot nothing. In some places the sky was opaquely visible through the glass. In others further visibility was blocked by the excreta of birds.

The Director appeared to be re-reading the note, then sat twiddling it in his fingers, giving the impression of a man in a state of very much agitated cogitation. He then handed it to his neighbour, the Editor. This character read it, and displayed precisely the same symptoms: the quick look upwards at the roof, followed by anxious re-perusal of the document. He and the Director then whispered together, after which consultation the Editor passed the note to Bagehot who sat next him. While the audience tittered at some jest uttered by Harrogate, Bagehot gave the impression of looking eagerly for somebody in the body of the hall.

The moment his glance fell on me, I saw him mutter something to the Editor, who in turn muttered to the chief Director. Bagehot then rose quietly, quickly and almost stealthily from his chair, and, stepping off the dais, reached the place where I was sitting. He thrust a sheet of paper, a sheet, I immediately noted, of our own hotel paper, into my hand.

'What d'you make of that?' he asked in a voice so strained and strange that I hardly recognized it as the one I had heard speaking so suavely in our lounge.

I looked first at the signature, which was on the second page. It was that of Irma. I then read the contents of the note itself. It stated that for reasons which certainly Mr Harrogate and Mr Buzbee would understand, she strongly objected to the sale of the Fitzpayne house for private profit, by which the children of the community would suffer. But since it was now too late to prevent this sale she must insist that Sun Hotels and, if they so wished, their associates, should make a large (this was underlined) contribution towards the purchase of alternative accommodation for the children concerned. She then named, in writing and in figures, the large sum considered requisite. The note concluded with the words 'As the bearer of this letter can testify I am at present on the roof of this structure, close to one of the open ventilators. In the event of my request not being met in the form of a cheque to be handed to my husband, Mr Ballantyne, who is in the hall, I propose to throw myself through the ventilator and fall to my death on your platform. This will be a happening which, I think, your best efforts will not be adequate to keep out of the press. Mr Bagehot has already indicated to me the adverse effects which bad initial publicity, and the aura of scandal, can have upon such a venture as yours.'

Since the letter was not only on our hotel paper but had clearly been typed on the typewriter in my office, it was obvious that Irma had brought it with her already written. While Bagehot stood trembling beside me, and the people on the platform who had read it looked in my direction with fearful anxiety, I glanced across the room at Farragut. He replied not only with a nod but with a sketchy thumbs-up sign.

'I suppose,' Bagehot was breathing into my ear, 'it's some sort of ghastly bluff.' He looked again automatically at the roof, an action followed by several prominent citizens seated near me. 'I don't see her up there.'

'Of course you don't you bloody fool,' I said, in a frenzy of anxiety. 'She's behind that mess of bird-shit. And if you think she's bluffing you don't know her.'

Bagehot whispered, 'Great God!' and went tip-toeing back on to the dais. Harrogate had by now finished his address, and the Editor was on his feet, welcoming Sun Hotels and 'all they stand for in the life of a better and brighter Britain'.

After a word to each from Bagehot, the chief Director, Harrogate and Buzbee got out of their chairs as unobtrusively as possible and, as I saw over my shoulder, were just leaving the dais as I myself hurried out of the side door followed closely by Farragut.

'She threw it down to me,' he said, hoarse with excitement. 'She's up there all right. There's an iron ladder for chaps to get up on to clean the roof. Christ, watch out!'

This scream of alarm was produced by the fact that the top of the ladder had been suddenly unhooked or otherwise detached from the roof, and the whole of it swung sideways and outwards, falling at its full length on the ground just as the platform representatives emerged from the side door.

Except for Buzbee they were babbling almost incoherently. Buzbee maintained a brooding silence, once reaching out to tap the branch of a tree growing close to the wall of the Crystal Palace and once, to my amazement, sketching a vague sign of the Cross on his chest.

In my agony of anxiety concerning Irma, I heard buzzing past and into my ears words and phrases such as 'Bluff', 'Outrageous', 'Blackmail', and even 'Fetch her down'. Then I heard my own voice raised in a kind of screech.

'It's not a bluff. You don't know her. She'll kill herself if you let her. If you try to go up after her she'll jump. It's true! It's true!'

The furious murmuring and occasional shouting – they were shouting up at Irma – continued in a dark, horrible haze of sound around me. The shouts met with silence from above. A hopeless silence fell momentarily on the group below. In this silence Buzbee spoke.

'I think, gentlemen,' he said, 'we have no alternative. We must, to put it in two words, pay up.'

'But, but but,' came from all around him. Someone said dubiously, 'She may have left a note, telling the whole story.' And somebody else said, 'What does it matter whether she has or hasn't? A suicide here and now can't be kept out of the papers. And it isn't going to do the hotel any good, whatever caused it.' And somebody else – Bagehot I think – said, 'It's a lot of money but it might be cheap at the price.'

My terror, thinking of what might happen to Irma, was such that I had the impression that the wrangle was going on for ever, though I suppose that in reality it cannot have lasted more than a few minutes. Then I heard, coming through a kind of dream fog, the voice of the Director saying, 'All right. I'll pay. I'll write a cheque.'

As though restored suddenly to life, I yelled the news up to Irma. Her voice came back, faint but firm.

'Tell them to give you the cheque and you take it to the bank and cash it. Otherwise they may stop it. I shall stay here till you get back.'

The Director handed me the cheque. I ran to the car. I drove with exaggerated caution, as though Irma's life was in my hands, to the bank. There was some delay while they assembled the large sum required in cash. I returned. I shouted up to Irma that I had the cash.

'Good,' she shouted back. 'Then get all those able-bodied louts down there to put the ladder back so that I can come down.'

Buzbee addressed me for the first time. 'Your wife,' he said, 'is a realist. I am so glad that there are not more like her in the world.'

Momentarily dazed by my dash to and from the bank, by the nearly incredible success of Irma's manoeuvre, I stood for a moment simply gaping at the grave, philosophic countenance of Buzbee.

Behind me there was a small commotion. I saw that the Director, Harrogate and Bagehot were jostling beside Farragut to get the ladder back into position. Their expressions were those of men who have been threatened with a curse, with some kind of witchcraft. It was as though the replacement of the ladder represented for them a sort of exorcism. Only by its means, and the return of Irma to earth, could they arrange their own return to normality. Struggling together for the common purpose, they got it up-ended against the roof. And in a collective, almost reverential shout they called up 'OK Mrs Ballantyne.'

Almost before I saw that in their superstitious haste they had the top of the ladder about four feet to the right of where it had been earlier, a good half-second before I had a chance to yell a warning, Irma came slithering down from her place on the roof, grabbed for the projecting top of the ladder, missed it, slithered right off the roof, turned over once in the air and hit the ground.

Rushing forward, I think I knew before I reached her that she must be dead. Even as she was falling I knew that nobody could fall from that height in that way and not be killed. I heard Harrogate and Farragut dashing back towards the hall shouting for a doctor, and knew that it was perfectly useless.

Behind me Bagehot was speaking hysterically.

'What'll this do to our project?' he kept repeating.

I heard Buzbee draw in his breath in a deep sigh. 'What'll this do to our project?' Bagehot wailed again. I heard Buzbee give a growl or snarl so savage that I looked round. Even at that moment there was room in my head for the thought that at least one story he had told of himself might be true. He looked less like a dishonest solicitor than a fighting man from the slums of Glasgow. Hardly moving his feet, he hit Bagehot a blow in the face so violent that, as Bagehot went down, I wondered vaguely whether Buzbee had killed him.

Buzbee stepped across and stood looking down at Irma. He groped above his head as though intending to take off his hat. He had no hat. After a moment's hesitation, he touched the top of his wig in a reverent gesture.

Whoever had been trying to keep the meeting going had by

now either lost the interest of the audience, or run out of steam altogether. The invited guests of Sun Hotels had poured out of the Crystal Palace and now stood startled, gaping and inanely twittering all around us. I had a violent sense that all the villains and idiots of the town were gathered about me. And then Buzbee spread his arms a little in the way he had, and seemed about to make a speech, or perhaps recite a stanza of his favourite poem. In a mindless reflex of rage I lashed out at him. I hardly knew what I had done. One moment he was standing there, and the next had staggered, tripped and fallen heavily backward. He sat up, and it was seen that his wig had been knocked off by his fall. The sight of him seated there, blatantly bald, seemed to strike those citizens dumb. They stared incredulously. Buzbee stared only at me. ' I warned you,' he said, ' I did warn you.'